The London Deception

Frank's nostrils flared as the smell of smoke reached him. He threw open the door to another dressing room. On the clothes rack, a woman's dress was ablaze.

Frank grabbed a pitcher of water and a handkerchief from the makeup table. Covering his mouth, he rushed toward the fire and tossed the water on it, but the fire had spread too far to be extinguished. Within seconds the whole rack of costumes was burning and smoke had filled the room. As Frank turned to run for help, the door to the dressing room slammed shut. He tried the doorknob and pulled, but the door didn't budge.

"Help!" Frank shouted at the top of his lungs.

He backed up and threw his weight against the door, but it held fast. Coughing, Frank sank to the floor, breathing in what little good air was left in the room through the handkerchief. His eyes fluttered as he began to lose consciousness and the fire continued to burn out of control.

The Hardy Boys Mystery Stories

Available from MINSTREL Books

THE HARDY BOYS®

158

THE LONDON DECEPTION

FRANKLIN W. DIXON

A MINSTREL®
BOOK

Published by POCKET BOOKS
New York London Toronto Sydney Tokyo Singapore

A MINSTREL PAPERBACK *Original*

A Minstrel Book published by
POCKET BOOKS, a division of Simon & Schuster Inc.
1230 Avenue of the Americas, New York, NY 10020

Copyright © 1999 by Simon & Schuster Inc.

Front cover illustration by Bill Schmidt

ISBN: 0-671-03496-0

First Minstrel Books printing September 1999

10 9 8 7 6 5 4 3 2 1

HARDY BOYS MYSTERY STORIES is a trademark of Simon & Schuster Inc.

HARDY BOYS, A MINSTREL BOOK and colophon are registered trademarks of Simon & Schuster Inc.

Printed in the U.S.A.

Contents

THE
LONDON
DECEPTION

1 A Trial in London

"Cold-blooded murder, m'lord?" the tall woman in the tweed suit asked. Frank Hardy watched from the balcony as the woman approached the judge's bench. "Look at that boy."

The woman pointed to Chris Paul, who was Frank and his brother Joe's English host for their two-week student exchange visit in London. Frank's brown eyes narrowed as he watched his thin, pale-skinned young friend shift nervously in his seat.

"He is only seventeen," the woman continued.

"Just like you," Frank whispered to his blond, blue-eyed brother sitting next to him. But Joe Hardy's nose was buried in a history textbook, and he wasn't paying attention.

"No matter how much he hated Professor Wick," the

woman went on, "he could not have bludgeoned him to death in the gymnasium."

A man suddenly strode toward the woman in the tweed suit. Grabbing her by the shoulders, he moved her two feet to the right. "I've told you ten times, Emily. You're blocking the audience's view of some of the business if you play the scene from there," Frank heard the man say to Emily Anderson, the actress playing the defense lawyer.

"Yes," Emily replied with her clipped, British accent, "but they get a far better view of me." The other cast members onstage chuckled, and Frank realized Emily was joking.

"Heads!" yelled a stagehand, and the seven actors in the cast immediately looked up and moved out of the way as a heavy piece of scenery was lowered by the cables of the fly system onto the stage. "Sorry for the interruption," the stagehand said.

"I'm sorry, Dennis," Emily went on with her conversation. "It feels terribly odd for me to be standing so far away from the judge at that point."

"Trust me, Emily, I'm the director," Dennis Paul replied.

Frank watched the director, who had the same pale skin and red hair as his son, Chris. Mr. Paul strode back to the edge of the stage, down the steps, and into his seat in the third row.

"Chris's dad sure is a perfectionist in rehearsals," Frank whispered to Joe. "I guess he must be under tremendous pressure, being the director and the

2

playwright. I don't know how he teaches full-time, too."

"Mmm," Joe replied, not looking up from his book.

"Earth to Joe," Frank said, tapping lightly on the side of Joe's head.

Joe finally looked over. "Sorry, Frank, I'm cramming for a history quiz tomorrow. Chris has been ribbing me that English schools are better than American schools ever since he came to stay with us in Bayport last year," Joe explained. "I'm going to prove him wrong."

"What does the quiz cover?" Frank asked.

"The Colonial Rebellion," Joe replied.

Frank furrowed his brow, puzzled for a moment.

"That's what Chris kiddingly calls the American Revolution," Joe explained. "It's strange, learning world history from another country's point of view."

Frank nodded, agreeing. He looked up at the ornate decorations on the ceiling and noticed the paint and the gold leaf flaking off from age and neglect. "This theater must have been incredible when it was built."

"You'd think in two hundred years, they might have gotten around to repainting it," Joe joked.

"Mr. Paul said this used to be a very fancy part of London," Frank explained, "but the whole area looks run-down now."

The Hardys' returned their attention to the stage.

"Most every student feared Professor Wick," Chris Paul said, now in the witness stand onstage. "He was cruel and unfair if he didn't like you, and he didn't like me."

As Frank watched Chris Paul working onstage with a

cast of professional actors, he felt proud, but envious of his young host.

"Think of it, Joe," Frank said quietly. "A week from now, this theater will be filled with an opening night audience and the London press. Chris is a year younger than I am, and as one of the stars of the show, he's going to be the center of attention."

"He's welcome to it," Joe said. "If I was on that stage in front of all those people, my stomach would be doing back flips. I'd be sweating bullets!"

Frank smiled, then added, "It must be exciting for Mr. Paul, watching his son make his theater debut."

"Probably the same way Dad felt when we solved our first mystery," Joe replied.

Frank nodded. As amateur sleuths, he and his brother were also following in their father's footsteps. Fenton Hardy had once been a police officer and detective and was now a private investigator back in the United States.

Joe heard a sound behind him. Turning around, he saw Jennifer Mulhall, the young technical director, popping out of the lighting booth at the top of the balcony and trotting down the steps of the aisle to the front row of the balcony.

Jennifer had short brunette hair and dark eyes. Although she was only about five foot two, Joe thought she radiated confidence and commanded respect from everyone on the technical crew. Noticing Joe watching her, she motioned him over.

Joe shimmied sideways down the row and followed Jennifer to the wall of the balcony.

4

"Spot me, will you?" Jennifer asked.

"Spot you?" Joe asked.

Grabbing on to an iron ladder fastened to the wall, she climbed up and motioned for Joe to follow.

They went up twenty feet, then Jennifer hopped off onto a catwalk. The narrow metal platform ran across the width of the theater behind a grid suspended from the ceiling. From the grid hung dozens of lights of various shapes and sizes. Joe looked down to the floor of the Quill Garden Theatre more than fifty feet below him.

"Don't worry, Joe, if you fall at least you'll end up with a good seat in the stalls," Jennifer assured him with a smile.

"The stalls?" Joe asked, not understanding.

"The orchestra section," Jennifer replied. "That's what you Yanks call it. Come on then."

Jennifer offered Joe a hand, and he carefully stepped onto the catwalk. "I guess you can't be afraid of heights if you're a technical director."

"You can't be afraid of anything," Jennifer replied, leaning far over the railing of the catwalk. "I need to adjust the focus on this Fresnel."

"What?" Joe asked, unfamiliar with the word.

"I'll show you," Jennifer replied. "Just be sure I don't topple over." Leaning farther over the rail, she tapped the side of the powerful light with her gloved hand until the light moved an inch or two to the left.

Joe watched the stage. Chris Paul, whose face had been partly in shadow, was now clearly illuminated.

5

"I see now," Joe said. "You hadn't aimed the light at the right spot."

"It was aimed right yesterday," Jennifer told him. "So either I didn't tighten the bolt well enough or the ghost has been at work."

"The ghost?" Joe wondered.

"The Ghost of Quill Garden," Jennifer replied. "She's been mucking about in this theater for more than a hundred years."

"A real ghost?" Joe asked, with a doubting smile.

"I don't believe in ghosts, either," Jennifer replied. "But I believe in her because I've seen her. I did a revival of *Pygmalion* two years ago. Late one night when I was working alone onstage, hanging lights on a truss I had lowered from the fly space above the stage, I saw this white figure floating across the catwalk above me."

"That's a long way up from the stage. From that distance, it would be hard to see," Joe pointed out.

Jennifer ignored him. "She didn't hurt me. She was just out and about for a stroll. I shut my eyes, and when I opened them she was gone."

"You'd been working with bright lights. Maybe when you first looked, your eyes were adjusting to the darkness," Joe offered.

"I told you what I saw," Jennifer said, shrugging. "The rest is up to you."

Joe and Jennifer watched rehearsal from the catwalk for a few moments.

"I can't believe I'm here," Joe said quietly to Jennifer.

6

"Yesterday, Frank and I were sitting in a classroom in Bayport. We flew out of New York City last night, and this morning we arrived at Heathrow Airport and took a train to Victoria Station. A double-decker bus took us to Islington, where we attended classes at a British school, and tonight we're at a rehearsal for the world premiere of a play written by, directed by, and starring our host family!"

"I tried to convince Dennis to give your visit a miss," Jennifer told Joe. "With the show opening so soon, I figured the last thing he needed was a couple of American teenagers knocking about his house. But he said you came highly recommended by your headmaster."

"Headmaster? Oh, you mean our principal," Joe translated.

"Right. He said you were good boys who never caused trouble," Jennifer recalled.

"Well, we are good," Joe agreed, smiling. "And I guess we don't *cause* trouble, but we sure have a knack for *finding* it."

"Something's not right," Jennifer said suddenly. "She's in shadow."

Joe peered down and realized what Jennifer meant. Emily Anderson had crossed to the edge of the stage and was no longer in the light.

Jennifer moved down the catwalk, then lay down on her stomach. "Joe, I need you to hold my legs. Would you mind?"

Joe nodded, stepped down the catwalk, and kneeled, holding Jennifer's legs while she stretched out under

7

the railing of the catwalk to adjust a light that hung lower than the others.

Frank watched how gracefully Emily Anderson glided across the stage toward Chris.

"I tell you that my client is an innocent victim," she stated firmly, placing a hand on Chris's shoulder.

Frank looked up from the action onstage to the lighting grid, shaking his head at Jennifer's daring.

"A little farther, Joe," Jennifer said, stretching out as far as she could and tapping on the side of the light.

Joe was pressed against the railing of the catwalk, gripping Jennifer by the ankles as she leaned on a lighting instrument. Suddenly the light directly across from her came on, shining an intense beam directly into her eyes.

"Hey! Who's in the booth?" Jennifer shouted, as two more lights came on full power.

"Hold a moment!" Mr. Paul called to his actors, and they all raised an arm to shield their eyes as they gazed up and out at the ceiling.

Frank turned and detected some movement out of the corner of his eye. In the light booth behind him, he thought he saw a figure in white moving behind the tinted glass.

Frank rose from his seat, ran up the steps, and flung open the door to the lighting booth. It was empty.

"No one's in the booth, Jennifer," Frank called.

"Bring down nine, fourteen, and seventeen!" she shouted to Frank.

8

Joe noticed two of the lights that had come on had begun to emit smoke. As he started to warn Jennifer, he saw that the third light, positioned directly over her head, was also smoking. "Jennifer, you've got to get back on the catwalk!"

One after the other, the huge bulbs inside the three lights exploded! Jennifer and Joe recoiled as glass and sparks shot out of a light above her head, showering down into the theater below.

Jennifer's left ankle slipped from Joe's hand. Still grasping her right ankle, Joe tried to brace himself against something and inadvertently placed his hand on one of the burning hot lights.

Joe instinctively drew his hand back. Jennifer's weight now pulled him through the gap between the two railings and off the catwalk. Hooking his knees around the lower rail, he scissored his legs and broke their fall.

Jennifer screamed as she was left dangling in midair, with Joe holding her by one ankle. Joe was clinging to the catwalk only by his legs. The weight of both their bodies was too much for Joe, and his legs began to slip!

2 The Ghost of Quill Garden

Jennifer's scream stopped Frank dead. Looking out of the lighting booth, Frank saw his brother hanging upside down from the catwalk, holding Jennifer by one ankle.

Frank feared he would never have time enough to climb up to the catwalk to save Joe before his legs gave out.

Spotting a coil of electrical cable in the booth, he grabbed it and hurried down to the front row of the balcony.

"Jennifer!" Frank shouted as he grasped one end of the electrical cable and flung the rest up toward the young lighting technician. She snatched the other end out of the air.

"Frank?" Joe called in a pinched voice, straining to

cling to the catwalk with his legs while maintaining his grip on Jennifer's ankle. If he didn't let go of Jennifer soon, he would lose his leg grip and they would both plummet onto the seats far below.

"Hang on!" Chris shouted from below.

"Wrap the cable around your wrist, Jennifer!" Frank called, while he looped his end several times around the balcony railing.

"Now what?" Jennifer called.

Just then Joe's muscles gave out and he lost his grip. He and Jennifer fell headfirst toward the audience below. Then, like jumpers attached to a bungee cord, their fall was abruptly broken as the electrical cable around Jennifer's wrist pulled taut. Joe flew past her, swinging from her ankle like Tarzan from a vine.

Joe's feet almost clipped the tops of the seats on the main floor of the theater. He and Jennifer swung up and down several times, then finally came to a rest.

Frank held firmly to his end of the cable with his back pressed against his seat and his feet braced against the short wall in front of the balcony's first row.

"Hold on, Joe, I'll pull you up!" he shouted, unable to look over the edge of the balcony to check on his brother.

"Don't sweat it," Joe called back as he let go of Jennifer's ankle and dropped three feet to the floor between two rows.

"Let go, Jennifer, I've got you," Joe said. Jennifer let go of the electrical cord and dropped into his arms.

"Jennifer? Joe? Are you sound?" Chris asked as he ran up with his father.

"If by 'sound,' you mean 'all right,' then the answer is yes," Joe replied.

"Now I know what it's like to be a trapeze artist," Jennifer added, shaking out the taut muscles in her arms.

"I'm just grateful that you're as *strong* as a trapeze artist," Joe said to her with a smile.

"Joe, are you two okay?" Frank called, having reached the orchestra section from the balcony stairs.

"Fine, Frank," Joe assured him. "Thanks to the life line you threw us."

"What happened?" a short, muscular man with a dark complexion asked Joe and Jennifer, as he and the other crew and cast members surrounded them.

"Three of the lamps blew, Neville," Jennifer explained. "Joe Hardy, this is my assistant, Neville Shah."

Frank saw a short, balding man with blond hair hurry in from the lobby escorted by Mr. Paul's stage manager, Corey Lista.

"Corey says there was an accident!" the balding man exclaimed.

"We blew three lamps, Mr. Jeffries," Jennifer explained.

"Three at once?" Jeffries exclaimed, turning angrily to Mr. Paul. "Are your people incompetent? The sparks from those lamps could have set fire to my theater!"

"I beg your pardon, Mr. Jeffries," Mr. Paul replied. "There must have been a power surge."

"But none of the other lights got brighter," Joe pointed out.

"Perhaps the computerized light board is on the fritz," Mr. Paul suggested.

"I had taken lights nine, fourteen, and seventeen out of the lighting plot all together," Jennifer countered. "They would have had to be turned on manually."

"Maybe they were," Frank offered. "I thought I saw someone in the lighting booth."

"Let's have a look," Jeffries suggested.

The Hardys and an entourage of cast and crew members followed Jeffries through the lobby and up the stairs to the balcony. Jeffries strode up the aisle steps to the lighting booth and threw open the door. "There's no one here."

"I know," Frank said, stepping up behind Jeffries. "The person must have gone out the door at the back."

Jeffries tried the door, then pointed to the dead bolt. "The door is locked, as it always is."

"Someone could have unlocked it with the key," Chris suggested. "Where does it lead?"

"To the back stairway," Jennifer replied.

"Only myself, Mr. Paul, and Miss Mulhall have the key to that door," Jeffries explained. "I was in the theater office downstairs."

"Mr. Paul was directing, and you know where I was," Jennifer added.

"So who did Frank see?" Joe asked.

"The Ghost of Quill Garden," Emily Anderson stated, her resonant voice carrying up to them from the stage, where she was seated at the defense table.

"Oh, not again," Jeffries grumbled.

13

"Was it a figure in white?" Emily asked.

"Yes!" Frank called back, his voice echoing.

"The acoustics are quite fine in this theater," Emily said in a normal speaking voice. "There's no need to shout, young man."

"Ms. Anderson, this is Frank Hardy and his brother, Joe," Chris told her.

"Oh, yes, the American exchange students," Emily recalled. "Welcome to our haunted theater."

"You saw Lady Quill, I'd wager," Corey Lista said to Frank.

"Who's Lady Quill?" Frank asked.

"She's no one," Jeffries said curtly. "She was the wife of the original owner."

"Lord Horatio Quill," Mr. Paul told the Hardys. "He owned most of the neighborhood a hundred years ago. Not an altogether sound gentleman. He caused quite a scandal among the nobility by allowing his wife to perform onstage."

"Why?" Joe wondered.

"The acting profession was considered beneath the dignity of a noblewoman," Emily Anderson replied with a wry smile.

"Lord Quill secretly planned to leave Lady Quill for another woman," Mr. Paul went on. "So as a final gift to ease her inevitable disappointment—"

"You mean, to relieve his guilt for being such a cad," Emily interjected from the stage.

"Yes, just so," Mr. Paul agreed. "In any case, in 1909, Lord Quill produced a revival of an Oscar Wilde play—"

14

"*A Woman of No Importance,*" Emily inserted.

"Yes, so it was," Mr. Paul said. "In any case—"

"A vanity production," Emily interrupted again.

Frank noticed Mr. Paul's face flush. He looked suddenly embarrassed.

"Emily, if you'd like to tell the story, please join us in the balcony," Mr. Paul said, his mouth tightening in a straight line.

"What's a vanity production?" Joe asked.

"It's a show that is mounted not because of the merit of the play or the talent of the actors, but because someone has money and wants to show himself off," Jennifer explained to Joe.

"Or show his *wife* off," Emily added.

"Reviewers look down their noses at vanity productions, so even if they are good, the reviews tend to be especially critical," Mr. Paul said.

"Are reviews that important?" Frank wondered out loud.

"Oh, yes," Mr. Paul replied. "They often spell success or failure for a play, and Lord Quill's production was no exception. The reviews tore Lady Quill's performance to pieces."

"And on that same night, Lord Quill told her of his plans to leave her," Emily said, staring straight into the fly space above the stage. "So she threw herself from a catwalk and fell to her death on this very stage."

"So now she haunts the theater," Lista added, "cursing other productions out of spite."

"If everyone believes the place is haunted," Frank asked, "why do you keep doing shows here?"

"Theater people love drama, Frank," Emily said. "And what's more dramatic than a haunted theater?"

"Stuff and nonsense!" Jeffries growled, turning to Mr. Paul. "Don't think you and Mr. Kije are going to use this to get out of your rental contract."

"Mr. Kije has every confidence that *Innocent Victim* will be a hit," Mr. Paul snapped back at the theater owner.

"I've heard it all before," Jeffries replied. "Then one day, the producer realizes the show's not so funny as he thought, or a star quits, and everyone gets the 'flop sweats.' Next thing you know, they're knocking on my door trying to break their rental agreement and blaming it all on this blooming ghost."

"I assure you, Mr. Jeffries," Mr. Paul said firmly, "this show will go on."

Jeffries huffed, turned, and left the balcony, grumbling to himself all the way down the stairs.

Frank studied the expressions on the faces of the cast and crew. They looked concerned, even fearful, and several private conversations were being muttered back and forth.

"We're all tired, I think," Mr. Paul said, sensing the mood of the group. "Let's call it a night."

"Right, everybody, actors are off tomorrow," Lista said in a loud, clear voice. "Crew call is nine to five."

As the group began to disperse, Joe glanced down at the stage. Emily Anderson was gone.

"Neville and I will stay behind to clean up, Dennis," Jennifer offered Mr. Paul.

"I'm sorry, I cannot," Shah said. "I will not stay in a theater with a ghost."

"Neville, even if this ghost exists, it's never tried to hurt anyone," Mr. Paul assured him.

Jennifer Mulhall raised her hand. "I beg to differ— Joe and I had to do a trapeze act to save our skins."

"And look at my broken wrist," Shah added, holding up his hand.

"You got that by falling off a ladder," Mr. Paul reminded the lighting assistant.

A thought struck Frank. Neville Shah could be about the same height as the short figure he'd seen in the lighting booth. "Where were you when the accident happened?"

"Me?" Shah asked. "In the light storage room off stage left. I was looking for gels."

"Gels?" Frank asked.

"You put them over the lights to create different colors," Jennifer explained.

"Can anyone verify that you were there?" Mr. Paul asked.

"Why do you ask?" Shah wondered.

"Well, you're one of the few people who knows how to operate the light board," Mr. Paul replied.

"Are you accusing me of something?" Shah asked, his eyes narrowing.

"Someone knew which control turned on the lamp beside Jennifer's head," Joe pointed out.

"Then you *are* accusing me," Shah said.

Corey Lista stepped over. "I'll be leaving now."

"Mr. Lista, where was I when the accident occurred?" Shah asked without taking his eyes off Mr. Paul.

"Backstage," Lista replied matter-of-factly. "I saw you run in from the wings."

"That's true," Chris agreed. "When I was looking for something to cushion your and Jen's impending fall, I saw Neville come from stage left."

Mr. Paul cleared his throat. "Well, I'm sorry if we implied anything. You're an excellent lighting assistant—"

"You do not need to apologize," Shah interrupted, "because I am no longer your lighting assistant. Right now, all that is broken is my wrist. So I quit before worse things happen."

With that, Shah walked away.

"Should I try to stop him?" Jennifer asked.

"No," Mr. Paul replied. "He seems to be quite decided."

"Strangely decided," Frank noted. "Like he was looking for a reason to quit."

Mr. Paul sighed. "Well, we'll simply have to replace him."

"For tonight, Jennifer, I'd be glad to help you clean up the mess," Joe said.

"So will I," Frank added.

"Thank you, that would be wonderful," Mr. Paul said. "Chris, why don't you stay, too, and see that Frank and Joseph get home safely."

Chris agreed, and Mr. Paul bid them all good night. While Chris cleaned up the glass shards from the main floor of the theater, Joe grabbed a wrench and helped Jennifer unfasten the broken lighting units.

Joe then handed the lighting instruments down to Frank, who was on a ladder in the balcony aisle.

As Frank took the second light from Joe, he noticed a shiny spot on one of the broken lamps. The spot was slippery to the touch. Rubbing his two fingers together, Frank realized it was some kind of ointment that had a faint oily smell.

"Jennifer, is there some reason to use grease on a lamp?" Frank asked.

"No, never," Jennifer replied. "Why?"

"The lamps' blowing may not have been an accident tonight," Frank told her. "It may have been sabotage."

3 The Unknown Saboteur

"Sabotage?" Joe repeated.

Frank showed Joe and Jennifer the traces of ointment. "It's some kind of tan-colored ointment."

"Looks like greasepaint," Jennifer said. "It's a type of stage makeup."

"Could grease paint rubbed on a lamp cause it to blow out?" Joe asked Jennifer.

"Yes," Jennifer replied. "Anything with fat or oil in it. The heat from theater lights is so intense, if the natural oil from your skin gets on one, it can be enough to make it blow."

"Who would have had a chance to tamper with these lights?" Joe wondered out loud.

"Neville and I are the only ones who have been handling them," Jennifer said.

"I think Joe and I ought to have a talk with Neville Shah," Frank said, then leaned over the balcony rail. "Chris, do you know where Neville lives?"

"No," Chris said and stopped sweeping up the glass. "I know in what direction he goes."

"He must be long gone by now," Joe said, frowning.

"No, I saw him leaving the theater with his satchel just a minute ago while I was emptying some glass into the dustbin," Chris informed them.

"If you're okay here, Jennifer," Frank said, "I'm going to take Joe and Chris and try to catch up with Neville."

Frank, Joe, and Chris exited the theater through the main doors. "He walks in this direction," Chris said, pointing to his right.

"But the subway station is that way," Joe countered, pointing to the left.

"We call it the *tube*, Joe," Chris corrected, dryly joking. "Or the underground."

"Tube, underground—it's still a subway," Joe joked back.

"Argue about it in English class," Frank said, slapping the other two on the shoulders and setting them moving in the direction Chris had pointed.

As they jogged, Frank checked his watch. It was eleven-fifteen at night. Other than some construction workers renovating a building across from the theater, the streets were nearly deserted.

"If this were New York City, the streets would still be buzzing with people," Frank noted.

21

"It's not like we're in Piccadilly Circus," Chris explained. "Quill Garden isn't a big tourist hot spot."

The boys reached a main intersection and stopped. Frank looked in all directions. There was no sign of Neville Shah.

"Sorry, mates," Chris said. "Don't know which way to go now."

Joe saw a pay phone across the street. "Do you have information here?"

"What sort of information?" Chris asked, confused.

"Directory assistance," Joe clarified.

"Oh, yes, of course," Chris replied.

Joe looked to his left. He saw no cars coming so he stepped off the curb.

"Look out!" Frank shouted, yanking Joe back by the collar of his shirt. A taxi sped by, honking its horn.

"Remember, Joe," Frank reminded him, "in London, you have to look right first."

Joe nodded. "I keep forgetting they drive on the wrong side of the road here."

"*We* drive on the wrong side of the road?" Chris piped in, ready to argue.

"Guys? Let's stick to finding Neville Shah," Frank reminded them. After looking right then left, they crossed the street.

"Anyone have a quarter?" Joe asked, quickly adding to Chris. "Twenty pence, I mean?"

Chris told Joe the number for information and Joe dialed. "Yes, could I please have the address for Neville Shah?"

"Shah is a very common East Indian name," Chris warned Frank and Joe. "We must hope there's only one Neville."

"One-seventeen Hayworth Place," Joe repeated the operator's information. "Thank you."

"Hayworth Place," Chris said thoughtfully, then nodded to the right. "I should think he would take this route."

"There's a bus stop," Joe pointed out.

Chris shook his head. "His home is just across the park. Most probably, he's on foot."

The boys set off running and soon reached the corner of a vast, wooded park that stretched as far as they could see in both directions.

"When you said park, you meant *forest*," Joe said.

"Yes, Victoria Park is quite large," Chris agreed.

"Do you think he would cut through the park this late at night?" Frank asked.

"I'm certain of it," Chris said.

"Why?" Joe asked.

"Because there he is," Chris replied, pointing toward a man near a statue at the entrance to the park.

"Neville!" Joe called.

Shah glanced back at them, then hurried into the shadows.

The Hardys and Chris hurried after him. Inside the park, Frank saw the silhouette of someone cutting off onto a side path lined with huge trees. "Come on!" Frank shouted.

Street lamps shed light along the path, but Neville

Shah was nowhere to be seen. "He couldn't have moved that fast," Joe said quietly. "He must be hiding."

"I'll go down the path, you two split up and go along each side," Frank instructed.

Frank walked briskly, scanning for any movement. Joe and Chris did the same, walking parallel to Frank outside the lines of trees. They checked out the bushes and behind every tree, but could find no sign of him.

"How did he get away?" Joe wondered. "This area is well lit, and we should have seen him."

"I'd like to know why he ran when you called him," Frank added.

"Maybe he does know something about the lights being sabotaged," Joe suggested.

Suddenly Neville Shah dropped to the ground behind them.

"Neville," Chris gasped, startled, "you'll give me a heart attack that way."

"Forgive me," Shah replied. "Thugs sometimes roam the park at night, so I climbed into a tree for safety."

Joe looked at the cast on Shah's arm and then up at the tree from which he had dropped. "How did you get up there?"

"I am a good climber," Shah replied. "Now, what did you mean by 'the lights being sabotaged'?"

Frank hesitated. Now that Shah knew what information they were after, it would be difficult to get him to slip up and admit anything. "Jennifer thought you might have seen something. We found traces of greasepaint on the blown lamps."

24

"Why would I want to do such a thing?" Shah reasoned. "I needed this job."

"Then why did you quit so quickly?" Joe asked.

"The ghost," Shah replied.

"The ghost is just a legend," Chris said.

"I saw her last night, floating near the lighting grid on the ceiling," Shah countered. "Now I know what she was doing."

"The ghost of Lady Quill coated the lights with greasepaint?" Joe asked skeptically.

"If you do not believe in ghosts, then I suggest you look to the actors," Shah said. "They are the ones who have use for greasepaint."

"Well, if you need the job," Chris said, "I know we need your lighting talents—if you change your mind."

"No, thank you. I have another part-time job to support me. Now good night, and good luck," Shah said as he walked off into the darkness.

As Chris and the Hardys headed back to the theater, they discussed the odd events of the evening.

"I've heard of one or two people claiming to see a ghost, but just about everyone who's stepped into the Quill Garden Theatre has seen this one," Joe said.

"I haven't seen it," Chris replied, "nor has my father."

"I saw someone or something in that lighting booth," Frank admitted, "but there are other possibilities I'd investigate before jumping to the conclusion it was a ghost."

"Like what?" Joe wondered.

"I would like to see exactly what's behind that locked

25

door in the booth," Frank answered. "Then I'll know more."

Back at Quill Garden, the Hardys and Chris ran into Jennifer Mulhall as she was about to lock up.

"Before you go, do you think you could just unlock the lighting booth for us?" Joe asked, smiling and nodding toward the chain of keys hooked to her belt.

"What are you boys up to, eh?" Jennifer wondered.

"We're looking for a ghost," Frank replied.

"Right. I'll just lend you the key," Jennifer said, thumbing through the dozen or more keys she carried. She hesitated.

Frank saw the concern wash across her face. "What's wrong?"

"Nothing," Jennifer said. "I'm just all in. Here's your key."

She unlatched the fastener, pulled a key off her chain, then refastened it. "Just leave the booth open and the key by the dimmer board. I'll get it in the morning."

"What about the main doors?" Chris asked.

"They're set to lock automatically from the outside," Jennifer explained. "So once you're out, you won't be able to get back in."

"Thank you, Jennifer," Joe said, smiling again.

"Cheers," she said, giving Joe a wink before leaving the theater.

Joe switched the red work light on in the booth. "Is that enough light?"

Frank nodded as he put the key into the dead-bolt

lock on the back door. After turning the key, he pushed on the door. It opened onto an old wooden staircase with dank, cracking cement walls.

"Not quite the crushed velvet and sweeping banisters they have in the theater lobby," Chris joked.

The stairs were dimly lit by bare lightbulbs. Walking down one flight, they came to a landing with another door.

"Wonder what these stairs are here for?" Joe asked.

"Dad said they renovated the balcony after a fire about thirty years ago," Chris replied.

"Maybe this used to be the only way to get to the lighting booth?" Frank guessed as he tried to fit his key into the dead-bolt lock on the landing door. "Sorry, no luck."

The boys continued down another flight that led them into a long hallway with a low ceiling. At the end of the hallway Chris stopped outside a door across from a short set of steps.

"We're beside the stage," Chris whispered, pointing to the steps. "That door leads to the stage left wing."

"Wing?" Joe asked.

"Where the actors wait to make entrances," Chris explained. "And where we store scenery."

"Where's the equipment room that Neville Shah said he was in when the accident occurred?" Frank asked.

Chris pointed to the door in front of them. Frank opened the door and saw a storage room filled with broad, deep shelves. Theater lights, some of which looked decades old, lined the shelves.

"I would say about thirty seconds passed from the time the sabotaged lights were turned on to the time Chris spotted Neville Shah coming from the stage left wing," Frank said.

"Yes?" Chris said, not following Frank's thinking.

"You're wondering whether Shah could have been the person you spotted in the booth and still have had time to appear on stage when Corey Lista saw him," Joe said, continuing his brother's thought.

Frank nodded. "Joe, you head up to the lighting booth. Chris, wait at the bottom of the stairway," the older Hardy instructed. "When I give the signal, Chris will yell for you to start—"

"And I burn rubber down here," Joe jumped in.

"I'll time you," Frank added as Chris and Joe headed back down the long hallway to the back staircase.

Frank yawned and stretched as he waited for the other two to reach their positions. It had been a long day—and night, he thought. Frank froze in mid-yawn when he saw someone's shadow on the wall of the stairwell leading to the stage. "Chris?" Frank called, turning his head.

"Yes?" Chris's voice echoed from down the hallway.

Frank turned back, but the shadow was no longer there. "Uh, nothing," Frank said.

"Joe has just started up the back steps," Chris called again.

"Okay. I'm going to check something out," Frank replied, pushing the bar to open the metal fire door leading to the stage.

One bare light bulb on a stand was the only illumination onstage. Frank heard a sound, something like a latch on a door closing. Across the stage he saw another metal fire door in the other wing.

He moved toward the door and opened it. Walking down some steps, Frank found himself in a hallway with many doors.

In the first room on the left, he flipped on the light switch and saw three chairs at a low counter. Mirrors above the counter were framed by light bulbs. Across the room stood a rolling coat rack hung with men's clothing. Frank recognized one of the costumes that Chris wore in *Innocent Victim*.

"A dressing room," Frank surmised. His nostrils flared as the smell of smoke reached him. He hurried down the hall and threw open the door to another dressing room. On another rolling rack a woman's dress was ablaze. A red candle and candleholder lay on the floor at the base of the costume rack.

Frank grabbed a pitcher of water and a handkerchief from the makeup table. Covering his mouth, he rushed toward the fire and tossed the water on it.

The fire sizzled but had spread too far to be extinguished. Within seconds the whole rack of costumes was burning and smoke had filled the room. As Frank turned to run for help, the door to the dressing room slammed shut.

Frank tried the doorknob and pulled, but the door didn't budge. Another dead-bolt lock, Frank realized, and someone with a key must have locked it from the outside.

"Help!" Frank shouted at the top of his lungs. "Joe, Chris!"

Frank backed up and threw his weight against the door, but it held fast. Coughing, Frank sank to the floor, breathing in what little good air was left in the room through the handkerchief. His eyes fluttered as he began to lose consciousness and the fire continued to burn out of control.

4 The Suspect Handkerchief

Frank barely felt the spray of water against his face as the sprinkler system in the ceiling came on. The door suddenly bumped against his head.

"Move, Frank, you're blocking the door!" Joe shouted, but Frank was too dazed to respond.

Joe reached around, using his muscular arm to push his brother out of the way. When he had the door fully open, he dragged Frank to safety.

"What happened?" Chris asked.

"Someone locked me in," Frank replied, still coughing from the smoke he had inhaled.

Joe peered into the still smoky dressing room, where the emergency sprinkler system had extinguished the fire. A single key stuck out of the dead-bolt lock.

"You two must have seen whoever it was," Frank

continued. "He would have had to pass right by you."

"We didn't see anyone," Chris replied.

"Unless there's a back way out of here," Joe added, helping Frank to his feet.

"There is an emergency exit," Chris told them.

"Then let's go," Frank said.

Joe stopped to jiggle the key from the lock of the dressing room, pocketed it, then followed Chris and Frank toward the back of the building. A red warning label on the door at the end of the hall read Emergency Exit—Alarm Will Sound if Opened.

As Chris pushed through the door, a shrill siren erupted in the hallway. Although Joe closed the door tightly once he was through it, the siren continued to sound.

"We've tripped the alarm," Chris told Joe. "Only the fire department or someone with the security code can turn it off now."

The emergency door led into an alley. Frank checked in both directions. "Whoever it was got away," he said in a low, downhearted voice.

"But not this way," Joe said. "The emergency siren would have already been tripped if he had come out this door."

"If he went the other way, he would have run into you and Chris," Frank pointed out, pocketing the handkerchief he was still carrying.

"Maybe she walked through the walls," Chris said.

"She?" Frank asked.

"The ghost," Chris replied.

"Are you being serious?" Joe asked.

Chris shrugged. "I don't know."

An hour later the Hardys and Chris stood in front of the Quill Garden Theatre, relating the story to some firefighters and a police detective inspector named Stuart Ryan.

"Who would leave a candle burning in a dressing room?" Detective Inspector Ryan wondered.

"Emily Anderson," Dennis Paul replied, suddenly appearing behind Frank and Joe.

"Who are you then?" Ryan asked.

"Dennis Paul," Mr. Paul replied. "I'm directing this show."

"We tried ringing you, Dad," Chris said. "No one answered at home."

"I was eating a late meal across the street," Mr. Paul replied, clearing his throat and returning his attention to Detective Inspector Ryan. "Emily has all sorts of superstitions she follows. She had a red candle burning in her dressing room when she had her first big success, so now she always has one burning for good luck."

"You allow her to leave it burning all night?" Detective Inspector Ryan asked.

"Not at all," Mr. Paul replied. "She must have forgotten to extinguish it."

The night air was chilly, so Frank put his hands in his pockets. He felt something and pulled out the handkerchief he had used to cover his mouth in the burning dressing room. A monogram was stitched into a corner of the cloth.

Bringing it close to his eyes to read the monogram, Frank smelled a familiar scent and noticed a large tan-colored stain on the handkerchief. Greasepaint, he thought to himself. The two-letter monogram read E.A.

"Well, whoever's to blame, it will cost a pretty penny," Detective Inspector Ryan told Mr. Paul. "The fire triggered the emergency sprinklers in the other dressing rooms as well. Some of your costumes were burned and the others were water damaged."

Mr. Paul sighed heavily. "That's a five-thousand-pound accident."

"We're not so sure it was an accident," Joe said. "Someone locked Frank inside that burning room."

"We've searched the premises," Detective Inspector Ryan said. "There's no one in the theater."

"You said yourself, Frank, no normal person could have escaped our detection," Chris noted. "Oh, and by the way, no one could have run from the light booth to the stage in twenty seconds. I timed your brother."

"Perhaps the dressing room door just got stuck," Detective Inspector Ryan offered.

"It was locked," Joe replied, pulling the dressing room key from his pocket, "with this key."

"Would Ms. Anderson have the key to her dressing room?" Frank asked.

"No," Mr. Paul replied. "Why do you ask?"

Frank showed them the handkerchief with the grease-

34

paint on it and explained about the possible connection to the sabotaged lights.

"Emily Anderson is a highly respected actress, and besides, Mr. Jeffries issued keys only to myself and Jennifer Mulhall," Mr. Paul told them.

"Mr. Paul, would you—" Frank began, finding it difficult to ask, "would you mind showing us your key to the dressing room?"

Mr. Paul shrugged, unoffended, and showed them the key that exactly matched the one in Joe's hand.

"That leaves Jennifer and Mr. Jeffries," Frank said.

"*What* leaves Jennifer and Mr. Jeffries?" Jeffries asked, walking up behind Frank.

"Mr. Jeffries, what are you doing here?" Joe was surprised.

"Well, since my theater was burning down, the police were gracious enough to contact me," Jeffries replied sourly.

"Do you have a key to the dressing rooms?" Frank asked Jeffries.

"Of course," Jeffries replied.

"Could we see it?" Joe asked.

"Who do you think you are?" Jeffries scoffed. "I don't have to answer to a young boy."

"I'd like to see it then, sir," Detective Inspector Ryan said with a tight smile.

Jeffries produced his key chain and showed them the matching key.

"That leaves Jennifer," Chris said to the Hardys.

"No," Joe said in her defense. "Anyone who ever

rented the theater and been issued keys could have had copies made before returning them to Mr. Jeffries."

"Didn't Emily Anderson mention another show she had done in this theater?" Frank recalled.

"The way I see it, Mr. Paul, you're just trying to cover up more bungling," Jeffries said. "One more bit of negligence, and I'll bring in my solicitor and close down the whole production."

"Mr. Jeffries, the only damage is to the dressing rooms," Mr. Paul explained. "Your insurance and ours will cover the damage to your theater, though I doubt it will help us replace all the costumes."

"What do you mean, Dad?" Chris asked.

"The man producing the show, Mr. Kije, purchased the cheapest insurance he could. I believe there's a three-thousand-pound deductible, so he'll have to pay out that amount to replace the costumes," Mr. Paul replied.

"Where is this Mr. Kije, anyway?" Jeffries demanded. "If he's a legitimate producer, he surely has access to that kind of money."

"Mr. Kije has told me he doesn't have another pound to invest in this production," Mr. Paul replied, bowing his head.

"Well, sink or swim, it makes no difference to me," Jeffries said, then turned to Detective Inspector Ryan. "Show me the damage."

The detective sent Jeffries into the theater with one of the firefighters.

"We'll be contacting Ms. Mulhall and Ms. Anderson,"

Detective Inspector Ryan assured Mr. Paul, then went back into the theater to continue his investigation.

Mr. Paul heaved another heavy sigh. "Let's get home, boys—we have a long day ahead of us."

A few minutes before midnight, the Hardys, Mr. Paul, and Chris boarded the last train of the night. On the tube ride home, the boys discussed the suspicious fire. "I'll feel better when Jennifer shows up with her makeup room key tomorrow," Frank said.

"You think Jennifer would try to burn down the theater?" Joe asked.

"Perhaps she just wanted to burn up Frank," Chris joked.

"But why?" Joe asked. "What motive would she have?"

"We don't know enough about anyone involved with this show to know *why*," Frank said. "But I think we'd better start finding out."

Frank could barely keep his eyes open in drama class the next day. Mr. Paul, who was his instructor, looked equally tired, as no one in the Paul household had gotten more than a few hours' sleep after the events of the night before.

"We'll start with a relaxation exercise today," Mr. Paul told his class, putting on a cassette tape of classical music. "I'm sure we could all use a bit of relaxation," he added to Frank and Chris.

Following instructions, Frank and the other students lay on their backs on the floor. Mr. Paul then directed them to relax their bodies a bit at a time, starting with their toes and working their way up.

By the time Mr. Paul told them to relax their eyes, Frank was fast asleep.

Meanwhile, Joe was surfing the Internet in the media center during his free period. After typing "Quill Garden Theatre" into the search box, he hit Enter. In a few seconds the screen revealed a list of sixteen entries. Most were reviews or publicity from past productions, but one listing was a magazine article about the sale of the theater.

Joe double clicked on the title, and read the details of the sale of the "haunted" theater five years earlier to Timothy Jeffries.

Joe found Frank leaving drama class, yawning wide as he apologized to Mr. Paul. "Sorry I fell asleep, Mr. Paul, I really was interested in doing the exercise."

"Why don't you borrow the tape," Mr. Paul said, handing him the cassette and a sheet of instructions. "You can do the relaxation exercise with your brother. It truly clears and refreshes the mind if you're stressed out."

Mr. Paul smiled, then moved down the hall.

"Hello, Joe," Chris said, coming out of the classroom. "Are those notes for your history quiz?"

"Very funny, Chris," Joe said, smiling and handing them a printout. "While you and Frank were sleeping through class, I was digging up information. Mr. Jeffries bought the Quill Garden Theatre five years ago. Seems the old owner thought it was haunted, too."

"'Of the thirty shows that have been in that theater in the last twenty years,'" Frank read aloud from the article, "'not one has been a hit.'"

"No one wanted to rent the theater any more because it was 'cursed,'" Joe said, pointing to another paragraph. "So the old owner sold it, cheap."

"I don't see the old owner's name," Chris remarked.

"The article says he wanted to remain anonymous," Joe told him.

"Wow, even *I'm* beginning to think this ghost is for real," Frank said, handing the article back to Joe. "I'd like some proof, one way or the other."

"Maybe this will help," Joe said, taking a folded piece of paper from his pocket.

Frank scanned the list of Quill Garden entries from Joe's net search. One entry was circled.

"Haunted London?" Frank said aloud to his brother.

"It's one of those walking tours for tourists," Chris explained.

"The Quill Garden Theatre is one of the haunted locations where the tour stops," Joe added.

"Paranormal historian James Bamberg leads the tour," Frank noted. "I've never heard of a paranormal historian, but maybe that's who we need."

"You meet your guide at seven P.M. outside the entrance to the underground at Tower Hill," Joe reported.

"Oh, you must see the Tower of London," Chris said. "That's where we keep our crown jewels. It's also the place where we locked up anyone no longer in power before beheading them."

"And even if Haunted London turns out to be a lot of baloney," Joe said, "it sounds like fun!"

"Are you up for it, Chris?" Frank asked.

"I have something to do later, but you two go ahead," Chris told them, then left for his next class.

That afternoon the Hardys walked to the underground station and waited for a train on the Circle line platform. As the train pulled into the station, Frank caught an unshaven man with dark hair peeking at him over the top of his newspaper.

Frank and Joe stepped into the car and sat down. When Frank looked at the man again, he was busily reading his newspaper and apparently paying no attention to Frank and Joe.

The Hardys took the tube to the Tower Hill stop and rode the escalators up to street level.

"Whoa, there it is," Joe said, pointing to a castle that loomed above the Thames River. "The Tower of London."

Inside the cobblestone courtyard of the castle, Frank and Joe decided not to take a guided tour and picked up a brochure instead.

"'Implements of torture,'" Joe read aloud from the pamphlet.

"Sounds like fun," Frank joked.

The Hardys followed the directions to one of the castle's four towers. Joe joined the end of a line of people passing by display cases filled with thumb screws, chains, and manacles, and even an executioner's ax.

Frank found the exhibit kind of creepy. Seeing a narrow stairway, he decided to explore a little. The stone steps spiraled upward to a landing about halfway up the tower. Here Frank found cells with cold stone floors.

Frank heard footsteps coming up the stairs behind him. "Joe?" Frank called back.

The footsteps stopped suddenly, and there was no response. Frank realized he was alone and saw no other exit from the tower. A chill ran down his spine.

Frank pushed his back against the wall at the head of the staircase and listened. After several seconds the footsteps resumed.

The unshaven man from the train stepped onto the landing, cautiously looking around. His trenchcoat hung open, and Frank caught a glimpse of a shoulder holster with a silver revolver.

5 The Surprise Investigator

When he saw Frank, the unshaven man closed his coat over his gun and smiled. "Hello," he said with a Cockney accent.

"Can I help you?" Frank asked.

"Help me?" the man asked.

"You've been following me ever since we got on the train," Frank accused.

"Not likely," the man replied.

"Yeah, you have," Joe Hardy said, coming up behind both of them on the stairs. "I saw this guy duck into the stairway a few seconds after you did and followed him."

"All right then, lads," the man said, pulling his wallet from his pocket. "The name's David Young. I'm a private detective." Young showed them his identification.

"Is that why you carry a gun?" Frank asked, handing back Young's identification card.

"Right," Young replied. "I sometimes have to trail dangerous characters,"

"But why are you trailing *us?*" Joe asked.

"Mr. Jeffries don't believe in ghosts," Young explained. "So he hired me to find out what 'living' people might be mucking about with his theater."

"And he thinks it might be us?" Joe asked.

"You're the blokes what were around when the trouble happened," Young replied.

"What motive could we possibly have?" Frank asked.

"You're friends with Dennis Paul," Young told him.

"So?" Frank said, shrugging.

Young paused before speaking. "Doesn't matter. From what I seen today and what I found out about you and your dad back in the States, I figure you're on the up-and-up."

"What do you know about us and our dad?" Joe demanded.

"That Fenton Hardy is a private detective of some reputation and that you are students at Bayport High in Bayport, New York," Young replied. "You have some fame as amateur sleuths and have helped crack a number of criminal cases."

"How did you find all that out so quickly?" Frank asked.

"It's the information age, eh?" he replied with a smug smile.

"You might try getting information on Emily Anderson," Joe said gruffly.

"Maybe I have done," Young shot back. "The police questioned her this morning. She claims she blew the candle out before leaving last night and says someone must have nicked her handkerchief from the dressing table and rubbed greasepaint on it."

"Nicked?" Joe asked.

"You know, nicked," Young repeated. "Stole."

"What about Jennifer Mulhall?" Frank asked.

"Jennifer Mulhall's dressing room key was missing from her chain," Young told them. "She don't know who might have taken it."

"Where was she last night when the fire broke out?" Joe asked.

"She claims she was home alone, but no one can confirm her alibi," Young replied.

"I have one more question, Mr. Young," Frank said. "If I was investigating this case, I wouldn't give up all that information to a pair of teenagers I had just met. Why did you?"

"Maybe we can help each other," Young explained, handing Frank his business card. "If you find out anything that might help me solve this business for Mr. Jeffries, give a call."

With that, Young gave them a nod and descended the steps.

"Wow, I guess Mr. Jeffries is pretty serious about solving this crime," Joe said.

"One thing Young said bothered me," Frank said, tapping his finger on the stone wall, thinking. "When we asked him what motive we could have for starting the fire, all he said was 'You're friends with Dennis Paul.'"

"So Mr. Young might think Mr. Paul had a motive?" Joe guessed.

"Or Mr. Jeffries might think so," Frank replied. "Until we know for sure, let's keep whatever we find out about the sabotage to ourselves."

Joe checked his watch. "Let's check out the rest of the Tower of London and then catch some supper before the haunted tour."

The boys viewed the Crown Jewels, an incredible collection of crowns, scepters, jewels, and jewelry that belonged to the British Royal Family.

After checking out the armor collection and the cells where some of the most famous and infamous people in history had been held, Joe and Frank grabbed a shepherd's pie for dinner at a nearby pub.

Dusk was falling on London by the time Frank and Joe returned to the rendezvous point for their tour. Frank counted a dozen people milling about in small groups, discussing their day—everything from Buckingham Palace to boat trips on the Thames.

"Ghosts!" a deep, booming voice suddenly rang out behind the group. As Frank and the others turned, one woman gasped. A figure stood on a low wall, wearing a black cape and white mask. "This city is full of them. My name is James Bamberg, and I tell you that all you need tonight to see them is an ounce of belief and seven pounds fifty in British sterling."

Joe and several others laughed when the guide's request for payment broke the tension. "We stop at the Quill Garden Theatre, right?" Joe asked as he handed over fifteen pounds to pay for him and Frank.

"You know about Lady Quill, do you?" Bamberg asked in return.

"We heard that she fell to her death from the catwalk above the stage," Frank replied.

"Fell? Pushed, I say—maybe by Lord Quill himself," Bamberg countered. "Yes, the cursed theater is our fourth stop, right after we take a breather at the Seven Bells Pub, in the neighborhood where Jack the Ripper once roamed."

After collecting the ticket fee, Bamberg held aloft a small white flag on the end of a rod and waved it. "Follow this and step lively."

Bamberg led Frank, Joe, and the other dozen tourists down narrow cobblestone streets and dark alleys, pointing out the ruins of the wall built around the city by the Romans when they invaded England two thousand years ago.

Bamberg paused in front of one ancient building, relating the legend of the spirit believed to be haunting the place, then led the group down cobblestone streets and narrow alleys to another and another.

"This guy sure knows how to creep you out," Joe whispered to Frank as they walked.

"Do you believe the stories?" Frank asked.

"I believe old buildings have a lot of history in them," Joe replied. "But not ghosts."

"After our next stop at the haunted chapel," Bamberg told the group, "we'll pause at the Seven Bells for some refreshment."

"The Seven Bells?" Frank asked.

"The very pub frequented by some of the victims of Jack the Ripper, and maybe even Jack the Ripper himself," Bamberg replied.

Inside the Seven Bells, Frank and Joe each ordered a ginger ale as they stood at the crowded bar beside Bamberg.

"What else can you tell us about the Ghost of Quill Garden, Mr. Bamberg?" Joe asked.

"It's our next stop, lads," Bamberg replied.

"Yes, sir, but Joe and I want to know a lot more than the others probably want to listen to," Frank explained.

"And why is that?" the guide asked, tilting his head back quizzically.

"We know the people doing *Innocent Victim*, the new show that's rehearsing in the theater," Frank explained. "Some odd things have been happening. A fire started mysteriously and I got locked in a dressing room. We're curious to find out how real this ghost might be."

"That's some serious business, lads," Bamberg remarked. "I will tell you a few things, but you're not to bring them up again during the tour. The Quill Garden has had a number of accidents in it, but so has every other theater. The real curse of the Quill Garden is its being in Spitalfields, an area that most tourists never go to."

47

"It seems like a nice enough neighborhood," Joe pointed out. "A couple of new shops have opened."

"Yeah, Spitalfields is on the rise, but there's nothing there yet that would be a big enough tourist draw to make the Quill Garden thrive. So the smarter producers with the bigger, better shows don't book the theater."

"And that's why there hasn't been a hit there in twenty years," Joe concluded.

Bamberg nodded as he sipped his pint of ale.

"So you don't believe the ghost of Lady Quill haunts the theater," Frank asked.

"Quite the contrary, lad," Bamberg replied. "I'm certain she does. But most ghosts don't do harm to the living. They slam doors, walk about in attics, and appear at windows. They don't start fires and lock doors."

Bamberg finished his pint and turned to the others. "Ladies and gentlemen, if you'd step outside, the tour will resume in just a minute."

Bamberg looked around the bar for something.

"One more question," Joe said. "We know the theater was sold five years ago to Mr. Jeffries, but who sold it?"

"Lord Quill," Bamberg replied.

"Lord Quill?" Joe repeated, looking at Frank in disbelief. "But he must have died years ago."

"Titles are handed down from generation to generation," Bamberg explained, bending down to look on the floor beneath the bar stools. "This was Lord Harold Quill, the grandson of the Lord Quill who built the theater."

"Why would he want to remain anonymous?" Frank asked.

"I suppose out of embarrassment," Bamberg replied without looking up. "The theater had been in the family for a hundred years, but it was such a terrible white elephant that Lord Harold sold it to Jeffries for next to nothing." Bamberg stood up, turned to them, and spoke rather sharply. "Now if you'd step outside with the others, I have some business to conduct with the pub owner."

Joe and Frank stepped out into the cold night air. A minute later Bamberg came out of the Seven Bells Pub and hurried down the street, calling over his shoulder, "All right, ladies and gentlemen, on we go."

Outside the Quill Garden Theatre, as Bamberg began explaining its strange history, Joe became aware of the distant sound of a power tool being used. He looked across the street at a building being renovated, but the place was dark and still. Then Joe realized the sound had to be coming from inside the theater.

"Corey Lista said the crew call was from nine to five today," Joe whispered to Frank.

Frank nodded.

Joe pointed to his watch. "It's eight-fifteen, and listen."

Frank and Joe stepped away from the group and Bamberg's booming voice.

Frank heard it, too. "Sounds like a drill or a screw gun."

"Stay with the group," Bamberg warned them, before

returning to his lecture. "It was right here in 1964 that the author of another ill-fated play was struck and killed by a lorry on opening night. The lorry driver swears he saw a figure in white standing over the body, then the figure disappeared."

"I want to find out who's in there," Joe said to Frank, nodding toward the theater.

"Now, if you'll follow me around the corner to the side alley, I'll show you the site of another strange incident," Bamberg said. As the guide led the group into the alley beside the theater, Joe and Frank peeled off and tried the front doors.

"Locked," Joe said, frowning. "Now what?"

"All the doors lock automatically from the outside," Frank said, "so I guess we knock."

Joe banged on the door, and the sound of the power tool stopped immediately. The boys waited for someone to come to the door. A minute passed and they knocked again, but no one came to answer.

"Let's check the stage door," Joe suggested.

Joe and Frank walked around the corner into the side alley. The tour group was nowhere to be seen, and the stage door was locked.

"We'd better catch up to the group," Frank said. "First phone we see, we'll call about someone being in the theater."

"But call whom?" Joe asked. "Jennifer? Mr. Jeffries? Mr. Paul?"

"Hard to know who to trust," Frank said, nodding. "I guess we call the police."

50

Joe spotted James Bamberg at the end of the side alley where it intersected with a second alley that ran behind the theater and the other buildings on Quill Garden Road. Bamberg had donned his mask again and was waving his white flag for the boys to follow. "Come on, Frank."

Joe and Frank hurried after Bamberg, but as they turned the corner into the back alley, they found it completely deserted.

"Look," Frank said, pointing to the mask and flag lying on the ground.

As Frank stepped forward to pick it up, Joe caught some movement out of the corner of his eye. A white hand in a second floor window pushed against the top of a wrought-iron gate leaning against the building.

The huge, heavy gate tilted forward and began to fall, with Frank standing directly beneath it.

Joe screamed to his brother. "Frank, look out!"

6 The Man in the Abandoned Building

Joe launched himself toward Frank, tackling him to the ground and rolling with him, just as the gate crashed onto the cobblestones behind them.

A woman across the alley leaned out of her apartment window. "Are you all right?" she asked, then went on without waiting for a response. "I've been telling them to haul that gate away before it fell on someone, and now look—"

"Excuse me, ma'am," Joe interrupted, pointing to the window where he had seen the white hand. "Who lives in that flat?" He remembered to use the word *flat* instead of *apartment*.

"No one lives in that whole building," the woman answered. "It's abandoned."

Frank had already moved to the back entrance, where

52

he noticed that the door frame was splintered where the door had been jimmied open, possibly with a crow bar. "Someone's pried open this door, Joe. Come on!"

Joe followed Frank into the abandoned building and up the stairs. The door to the second floor apartment on the alley was open, but no one was there.

They rushed up the central hallway and down the stairs to the main entrance, but the lock on that door was still in place. "Maybe he headed for the roof," Joe suggested as he led the way back up the stairs.

As the boys reached the door to the roof, Frank again saw that the door had been jimmied open.

Pushing it open, Frank and Joe searched the roof of the abandoned building. On the roof was scattered debris—scraps of lumber, broken glass, and roofing material, but the Hardys found no sign of the person Joe had seen in the window.

Frank looked over the low wall that ran around the perimeter of the roof, but saw no ladder or any other means of escape.

"I don't get it," Frank told Joe. "How does this person keep eluding us?"

"Unless he or she is a ghost," Joe said.

Frank saw a metal shaft sticking out from some debris and pulled it out. "A ghost who uses a crow bar?" Frank said, showing Joe the tiny splinters of wood stuck to the prying end of the bar. "Maybe it's someone who wants us to *think* he's a ghost."

The boys descended the stairs and left through the rear door. Outside, James Bamberg was waiting, his face red, his expression angry. "Where did you lot go?" he asked the Hardys. "And what do you mean by nicking my mask and guide flag?" he added, pulling the crumpled mask and broken rod from beneath the fallen iron gate.

"We didn't take them, Mr. Bamberg," Frank told him.

"I gave the owner of the Seven Bells the what for," Bamberg went on. "I thought one of his customers had nicked them."

"Someone wearing that mask and using that rod lured us into a trap," Frank said.

"I've been with the tour group," Bamberg insisted, pointing a thumb over his shoulder. "Ask them. I only left them half a minute ago to come searching for you two."

"Then it must have been someone at the Seven Bells who took it," Joe deduced. "That means whoever tried to knock you off has been following us this whole time."

"Knock him off?" Bamberg repeated, confused.

"Maybe David Young, that private investigator, never stopped following us," Frank guessed.

"You need to speak with a constable," Bamberg said. "And I need to rejoin my group. If you want to wait in front of the theater, I'll ring the police and send them over."

When Detective Inspector Ryan arrived and listened to the Hardys' story, he acted rather callous about the whole thing. "We get reports approximately once a month about strange sounds in this theater."

"What about the iron gate that almost turned Frank into a waffle?" Joe asked.

"We get reports *twice* a month about homeless men sleeping in that abandoned building," Detective Inspector Ryan replied. "You probably frightened one of them, and he knocked the gate over by accident."

"Knocked it over by accident? That gate weighs five hundred pounds," Frank insisted.

"Boys, I'll look into it," Detective Inspector Ryan said with an impatient sigh. "Now, why don't you two get home to bed."

By the time the Hardys returned to the Pauls' home, it was nearly ten P.M.

"I had begun to think one of the ghosts of Haunted London had done you in," Chris joked.

"That's not far from the truth," Frank said, and retold the story of their evening.

"Granted, it sounds like someone has it in for you two," Chris agreed. "But how could he be inside using power tools one minute, and outside wearing the guide's costume the next?"

"We're not sure," Frank admitted.

"Somebody had to have followed us into the Seven Bells," Joe pointed out, "so there may be an accomplice."

Just then Mr. Paul walked in, looking glum, his head bowed.

"Dad, where have you been?" Chris asked.

"Meeting with Mr. Kije," Mr. Paul replied. "The costumers needed half the money in advance."

55

"Frank and Joe had another weird encounter outside the Quill Garden—" Chris began to tell him.

"Doesn't matter, Chris," Mr. Paul interrupted. "Mr. Kije can't raise any more money. He's going to cancel the show."

Chris's face dropped, and Joe put a comforting hand on his shoulder.

"I've had Corey call a special meeting with the cast and crew tomorrow morning to tell them," Mr. Paul said wearily.

"What about school?" Chris asked.

"Another teacher is covering my classes," Mr. Paul replied. "The headmaster knows we won't be there," he added, then headed up the stairs to bed.

Joe and Frank stayed up another hour, whispering.

"I feel bad, not telling Chris about the private detective that Mr. Jeffries hired," Joe said.

"But what if Mr. Jeffries is right to suspect Mr. Paul?" Frank conjectured. "What if Mr. Paul and Mr. Kije are afraid the show is going to flop and are trying to create reasons to break the contract with Mr. Jeffries and get their rent money back?"

"You've watched Mr. Paul in rehearsal," Joe insisted. "He wants *Innocent Victim* to go on more than anyone."

"I've also noticed that he suddenly appeared after the fire in the dressing room, saying he had been eating a late meal," Frank reminded Joe. "And he could have been there tonight when the gate almost fell on me."

"He said he was meeting with Mr. Kije," Joe said. "Maybe it's Mr. Kije we need to investigate."

"For the sake of Chris and the show, I think you and I had better get permission to miss school tomorrow, too," Frank suggested before saying good night and rolling over to sleep.

The next day the Hardys, Chris, and Mr. Paul stopped to grab breakfast at the Lamb and Wolf, a pub just down the street from the Quill Garden Theatre.

Joe watched Mr. Paul, who stared blankly out the window, clearly crestfallen by the announcement that he would soon be making to the cast and crew of the show.

Chris checked his watch and suddenly got up from the table. "I'm not hungry. I'll see you all at the theater."

"What's up with Chris?" Joe wondered.

"With all the trouble, it's no wonder he's anxious," Mr. Paul replied.

Frank watched their red-haired friend through the window as Chris hurried down the street. Quill Garden Road bustled with activity. A new café had a Grand Opening banner hanging over the entrance, and the construction crew was working full tilt on the building across from the Quill Garden.

"Do you know what that's going to be?" Frank asked Mr. Paul.

"What?" Mr. Paul asked, preoccupied. "Oh, it's going to be one of those multiplex cinemas you Americans are so fond of."

Joe noticed a white limousine pulling up outside.

Two men, one with close-cut black hair and the other with a frizzy mass of blond hair, stepped out of it.

A commotion erupted by the door as patrons of the pub rose from their seats and crowded around the man with frizzy hair. The black-haired man politely pushed the crowd away from the blond man, then they took a seat together in one of the booths.

"Is he a rock 'n' roll star?" Joe asked Mr. Paul.

Mr. Paul looked over his shoulder. "Bigger than a rock star, he's a footballer."

"A footballer?" Joe asked.

"A soccer player," Mr. Paul explained, seemingly unenthused. "John Moeller—he's a superstar right winger for West Ham United."

"Wow, I've never seen a soccer player get that kind of reaction," Frank said.

"In Europe it's as big a sport as American football, baseball, or basketball," Mr. Paul explained. "And its heroes are like royalty."

"A soccer match in England," Joe said, grinning at the idea. "Now, that's something I'd love to see."

"If you come back in six months, you can see him play in the World Cup," Mr. Paul told him. "England is hosting it this year."

Mr. Paul fell silent again, sighed heavily, and stared out the window. Joe could tell it was taxing him to make conversation, so they ate the rest of their meal in relative silence.

When the Hardys and Mr. Paul walked into the theater lobby a little while later, Corey Lista was waiting.

"I have the cast and crew assembled, Mr. Paul," Lista said, then referred to a sheet on his clipboard. "They're all here except for your son and, of course, Neville Shah."

"Thank you, Corey," Mr. Paul responded, trying to smile.

Joe saw Emily Anderson on the pay phone at the far end of the lobby and casually walked over to check out the show posters adorning the wall.

"The show may not go on after all." Joe overheard her saying in a hushed voice. "I'll know for sure after this meeting, Ian. You have to stall Schulander for another day."

Emily noticed Joe standing nearby and raised her voice. "I'll ring you up after rehearsal then, yes?"

Hanging up the phone, Emily smiled sweetly at Joe before walking into the theater.

"Mr. Paul!" Joe heard someone call. The ticket clerk hurried out of the box office, holding an envelope. "Mr. Paul, someone left this on the counter," the clerk said, handing it to him. "It's addressed to Mr. Kije."

"'From an anonymous donor,'" Mr. Paul read the outside of the envelope aloud before opening it.

As Joe walked beside him, Frank leaned over and whispered. "That's a strange way to invest in a show."

Mr. Paul pulled a check from the envelope, then gasped. "It's a bank check for three thousand pounds."

7 The Anonymous Donor

"Three thousand pounds?" Frank said quietly to Joe. "Exactly how much Mr. Paul said he needed to save the show."

"Who did you say left this?" Mr. Paul asked the box office clerk.

"I don't know. I didn't see anyone," she replied, then returned to her post.

"Well, boys," Mr. Paul said, smiling genuinely, "maybe we're not closed yet after all!"

As the Hardys followed Mr. Paul into the theater and down the side aisle, Joe ran into Jennifer. Joe felt oddly embarrassed encountering his new friend, who had become a suspect since the last time he saw her.

"Where were you today, Joe?" Jennifer asked. "We haven't had one disaster, it's been dull as dirt."

"You heard about the fire the night before last?" he asked.

"Heard about it?" she replied. "I had the police knocking on my door at two o'clock in the morning."

"You think someone stole the dressing room key from your chain?" Joe asked.

"Someone must have," Jennifer replied, "but I don't know how."

"Have you ever used the key?" Joe asked.

Jennifer shook her head.

"Maybe it was never on the chain." Joe went on. "Who issued you your keys?"

"Mr. Jeffries," she replied.

Frank had stopped to listen and decided to try to provoke a reaction from the young technician. "What were you working on in here last night, Jennifer?"

Jennifer wrinkled her forehead. "I wasn't here," she replied, puzzled. "And the crew knocked off about five-thirty."

Joe frowned at Frank. He knew his brother had tried to catch Jennifer off guard and let something slip, but Joe felt sure she wasn't involved. "We heard *someone* in here using power tools at about eight last night."

"Don't know, Joe," Jennifer replied with a shrug. "I locked the place up when I left."

"Jennifer, this concerns you, too," Mr. Paul called from the stage, where he had assembled the cast and crew.

"If you're dropping the ax on this show," Emily said loudly to Mr. Paul, "can we get on with it?"

As Jennifer started toward the stage, Joe held Frank back a moment. "Instead of questioning Jennifer, why aren't we talking to Emily Anderson?"

"I don't see Ms. Anderson scaling ladders and escaping from rooftops," Frank replied, watching the refined older woman elegantly pacing across the stage. "Besides, why would the star of a show try to sabotage it?"

"I overheard her on the phone telling someone named Ian to stall someone named Schulander until she found out whether this show was being canceled," Joe informed him.

Frank raised an eyebrow. "That *does* sound suspicious."

Chris came running down the aisle on the other side of the theater. "Sorry I'm late!"

"All is forgiven today, Chris. An anonymous donor has given us new life," Mr. Paul said, then turned to his stage manager. "Corey, if you would run the scene at the headmaster's office with Emily and Chris, I need to deliver this check to Mr. Kije and get the deposit to the costumers."

"Can't you just send someone?" Lista asked.

"No, this I need to do myself," Mr. Paul replied, then hurried from the theater.

"Well, if we want to find out about Mr. Kije, here's our chance," Joe whispered to Frank.

"Say, Joe, I need someone to run a spotlight until we get a replacement for Neville," Jennifer called as she started up the steps.

"I'll trail Mr. Paul," Frank said quietly.

"What should I do?" Joe asked.

"Find out what you can about Emily Anderson," Frank replied. "And learn how to work a spotlight," he added with a smile, then hurried to catch up with Mr. Paul.

Frank followed Mr. Paul at a safe distance, expecting him to hop on a bus or flag down a cab to take him to Mr. Kije's home or office. Instead, the director and author walked a few blocks and went directly into the First Merchants Bank of England.

Maybe Mr. Kije is a banker, Frank thought, as he stepped through the revolving doors into the bank lobby.

Mr. Paul stood in the single line for the tellers. Grabbing a London *Herald* someone had left on a counter, Frank sat in the customer service waiting area watching Mr. Paul over the top of the newspaper.

Chris's father had reached the front of the line. The man behind him tapped him on the shoulder and pointed to an available teller, but Mr. Paul shook his head no and pointed toward a young female teller at a different window.

From the way the young female teller greeted Mr. Paul when he reached her window, Frank could tell they knew each other, although he couldn't hear what was being said.

Frank watched as the young woman took the cashier's check and began counting out money on the counter. Frank could tell they were large denominations because of the physical size of each bill. He knew that in England, the larger the bill, the more it was worth.

"Something smells a bit fishy, eh?" someone across the waiting area from Frank said. It was David Young, the private investigator.

"Maybe she thinks he's Mr. Kije," Frank said quietly.

The teller handed Mr. Paul the money in a large envelope and added, "Have a lovely day, Mr. Paul."

"Or maybe she doesn't," Young said.

Frank drew the newspaper in front of his face as Mr. Paul passed him and left the bank.

"Someone followed us last night after we left the Tower of London," Frank said, waiting for Young's reaction.

"By your tone, I fancy you think it was me," Young said. "Since I left you and your brother, I've been trailing Dennis Paul."

"Then you must have been there when he met with Mr. Kije last night," Frank said, seeing a chance to get an address for the mysterious producer.

"I followed Dennis Paul to half a dozen quite luxurious homes in Kensington and Mayfair," Young told him. "He stayed between ten and thirty minutes at each. I checked the addresses and none of the residences, I assure you, was Mr. Kije's."

"Then Chris's father lied to us," Frank realized.

"Don't be fooled just because he's someone's father," Young said. "Many criminals are, you know."

"Thanks for the tip, Mr. Young," Frank said, rising. "Can I ask you something? Did *you* tell anyone about our whereabouts last night?"

"I reported to my employer," Young replied, rising from his chair. "Told him you were no longer suspects in my book."

"Your employer, Mr. Jeffries," Frank recalled.

Young nodded, bid Frank goodbye, and left. As Frank headed down the street back toward the theater, his mind raced, trying to fathom why the author and director of *Innocent Victim* might be trying to sabotage his own production.

Meanwhile, Joe was high up on the catwalk practicing following Chris Paul around the stage with a spotlight four feet long and as thick as a tree trunk.

"Steady, Joe, move smoothly," Jennifer instructed over his shoulder. "Now pick up Emily crossing down stage center."

"Do you know a friend of Ms. Anderson named Ian?" Joe asked as he tilted the spotlight so that the beam stayed on Emily Anderson as she moved toward the edge of the stage.

"Ian Link," Jennifer replied. "But I don't think he would count as a friend. He's her agent."

"She was talking with him about someone named Schulander," Joe said. Jennifer's head cocked back, surprised. "You know him?"

"Joe, you're shining the spotlight on Corey Lista, in the third row," Jennifer warned.

"Sorry," Joe said, aiming the beam at Emily Anderson again.

"I don't know Schulander personally, but everyone knows *of* him," Jennifer explained. "He's a big producer in the West End."

"West End?" Joe asked.

"London's version of Broadway," Jennifer answered. "Schulander's been holding auditions for his new show these past two weeks.

"That's the motive!" Joe blurted out as a thought struck him.

"What's the motive?" Jennifer asked.

Joe hesitated, not wanting to give her too much information. "In the play, I just figured out the killer's motive."

"Your second day at rehearsal and it's just come to you, has it?" Jennifer kidded.

"Jennifer, can I borrow Joe for a minute?" Frank asked, having returned and stepping out onto the balcony below them.

Jennifer nodded for Joe to let her take over. "Go on then."

Frank led Joe through the red velvet curtains and into the lounge on the balcony level. He quickly filled him in about the bank and his encounter with David Young.

"Mr. Paul just cashed that check written out to Mr. Kije," Frank told him.

"Cashed it?" Joe asked.

"The bank teller may be involved," Frank explained.

"She knew who he was and gave him the money anyway!"

"You think Mr. Paul is pulling a scam?" Joe wondered.

"That's what it looks like," Frank replied. "We need to find out if Chris told his father where we were going last night."

"And don't forget Mr. Jeffries," Joe said.

"Right," Frank agreed. "If David Young reported our whereabouts to him, he could have followed us, too. But why would Mr. Jeffries hire an investigator to solve a crime that he was involved in?"

"Then again, what motive could Mr. Paul have?" Joe asked.

Frank shrugged. "Motive is the key to solving this one, Joe."

"Maybe Mr. Paul and Mr. Kije have a joint account at the bank," Joe suggested.

"Maybe," Frank said. "Let's wait and see what Mr. Paul does with the money."

"Speaking of motive," Joe told Frank. "There is a reason the star might try to sabotage her own production—if she was offered a bigger, better show." Joe then reminded Frank about the phone conversation he had overheard. "She would have a lawsuit on her hands if she walked away from this show a week before opening," Joe theorized. "But if the show were canceled, she wouldn't be breaking her contract."

"But could any job offer be big enough to make

someone with Ms. Anderson's reputation resort to sabotage?" Frank challenged.

"All right, cast!" Mr. Paul's voice rang through the theater. "Let's run through the show from the top."

Joe and Frank stepped onto the balcony.

"Joe, I need you back up here," Jennifer called from the catwalk. "Frank, would you be a love and get me two number forty-seven orange gels from the light storage room?"

"Sure, Jennifer," Frank replied, then trotted down the steps, through the theater, and into the stage left wing.

Emily Anderson had already begun her opening soliloquy, lit only by a spotlight. Frank paused, watching her from the wings. However brusque she could be in person, Ms. Anderson was mesmerizing onstage, drawing you in with her melodic speaking voice and commanding presence.

Beside Frank a stagehand wearing a wireless headset turned to the technician manning the fly system behind him. "Get ready to fly out the courthouse facade."

Chris stepped up beside Frank, ready to make his entrance. "How do you like being back here with us?" he whispered.

Frank smiled.

Just as Emily Anderson finished her speech, the stagehand beside Frank gave the cue. "Fly out courthouse, set classroom."

Frank watched as the huge set piece was raised high into the air.

"Why isn't Emily moving?" Chris muttered.

Frank saw that Emily Anderson hadn't moved from the spot where she delivered her opening speech.

Chris shrugged, puzzled, then walked onstage and took a seat at a desk in the classroom.

Frank heard a cracking sound from above him. The massive courthouse set piece was giving way directly over the spot where Chris Paul had just sat down!

8 A Major Setback

"Heads!" Frank shouted, remembering the warning he had heard shouted a couple of days before.

Chris looked up just as the giant set piece broke away from the cables that were lifting it. He leaped away from his desk a split second before the courthouse facade crashed down on top of the classroom set, tearing through the walls and sending desks splintering in every direction.

A violent crash of metal behind Frank sent him diving to the floor. The counterweights that had been balancing the one-ton courthouse crashed into the rigging at the base of the fly weight system.

Screams and gasps were followed by a shout of concern from Mr. Paul as he jumped onto the stage and ran to his son. "Is everyone all right? Is anyone hurt?"

"I'm fine, Dad," Chris assured him, then turned to Frank. "Are you all right, mate?"

Franks ears were ringing, but he was otherwise in one piece. "I'm okay."

"In case you're interested, Dennis, I am also uninjured," Emily said from the other side of the stage.

"The ghost has it in for this play," Corey Lista snapped, stepping up to Mr. Paul, his brow furrowed in anger. "I'm not hanging about to see what she does next."

Frank checked out the courthouse facade. The cleats that had attached the set piece to the steel cables had been torn away from the top of the frame, revealing numerous screw holes in the wood where the cleats had been secured.

Frank noticed a few larger holes where the wood had splintered as the screws were torn out by the falling weight, but most of the holes were small and smooth. Frank looked around the stage floor for loose screws that had been dislodged but could only find three.

"Frank!" Joe shouted as he ran up to his brother's side.

"I'm fine, Joe, but check this out," Frank said, showing him the three screws. "I have a hunch most of these screws were removed," Frank explained. "The few screws that remained couldn't bear the weight and tore loose."

"More sabotage," Joe concluded.

"What happened, Frank?" Jennifer asked as she stepped up to survey the damage.

71

Joe started to open his mouth, but Frank nudged him to stay quiet. If Jennifer were responsible, Frank figured she might try to hide the truth. "We don't know," Frank answered Jennifer. "What do you think?"

Jennifer looked at the top of the frame, then high up into the stage house where the steel pipe that had held the piece still dangled. "It looks like it was deliberate. Someone pulled the screws."

Joe nodded to Frank, satisfied

"Corey, you can't quit over a ghost!" Mr. Paul argued with his disgruntled stage manager.

Joe and Frank stepped up behind Lista. "Chances are it wasn't a ghost," Frank interjected, then explained what he had discovered and what he thought it meant.

"Whether it's a ghost or incompetence or sabotage, I'm not risking my skin another day here!" Lista fumed.

"You have to give me two weeks notice so that I can replace you," Mr. Paul pleaded with him.

"My union allows me to walk immediately if working conditions are unsafe," Lista replied firmly, handing Mr. Paul the stage manager's prompt book. "These conditions aren't just unsafe, they're deadly."

Lista stormed off the stage, passing Timothy Jeffries in the aisle. "Good heavens, now what?" Jeffries exclaimed, scowling at the sight of the wrecked scenery.

Frank noticed Emily Anderson sitting off to the side away from the action and recalled Chris's concern that she hadn't moved as she had been directed a moment before the set piece fell.

"You sure are lucky you stayed down on the edge of the stage, Ms. Anderson," Frank said, acting concerned so that his words wouldn't sound like an accusation. "If you had gone to the classroom, you might have been badly hurt."

"Yes, Emily, that's right," Mr. Paul said, having had his memory jogged by Frank's comment. "Why did you change your blocking?"

"I felt it would be more effective to stay downstage until the scene was fully set, and then walk into it," she replied, undaunted. "So I tried it."

"You have to admit, it does seem a bit suspicious," Mr. Paul said.

Emily rose to her feet. "I don't have to admit anything," she said icily, then walked off the stage.

"It appears you have a mutiny on your hands, Mr. Paul," Jeffries remarked.

As Joe watched Emily Anderson storm up the aisle, his eye caught some movement in one of the private box seating areas. The curtain behind the plush chairs had been pulled aside. A face was peeking through, but the moment Joe focused on it, it disappeared.

"Someone's behind that curtain!" Joe called to the others.

"Show yourself, whoever you are!" Mr. Paul shouted. No one responded.

Joe jumped off the stage. "How do I get to those seats?" he yelled over his shoulder.

"I'm sorry!" a voice above him called out. A man in a work shirt and tool belt stepped timidly through the curtain of the private box. "I heard the crash and peeked in—it's none of my business."

"What *is* your business?" Mr. Paul demanded.

"I'm an electrician," the man replied. "I was just—"

"He's an electrician, I can verify that," Jeffries interrupted. "After the incident with the lights, I wanted to be sure there wasn't a problem with the electrical wiring in the theater."

"Would you mind showing us your identification?" Joe asked.

"Why, you impudent little—" Jeffries snapped at Joe.

"I don't mind," the electrician replied, and dropped his wallet down to Joe.

Jennifer verified that his identification card was in order, then tossed the wallet back up to the electrician in the box. "So, was there a problem with the wiring?" Jennifer asked.

"No, it's installed to B.S.I. standards," the electrician replied. "You've passed inspection."

"Thank you," Jeffries said to the electrician. "If you'll meet me in my office, we can conclude our business." Jeffries now turned to Mr. Paul. "As for you and this circus of bungling fools you call a show, I don't want any actors on the stage until everything is fully repaired. If one of their union representatives saw this—"

"I know, they might close down our show," Mr. Paul said.

"Worse, they would give me a hefty fine," Jeffries concluded before heading back to his office.

Mr. Paul turned to his son, patted him on the back,

then turned to the rest of the group. "Ladies and gentlemen, this may be the final straw. We don't have the money to hire the stage carpenters to rebuild the set. Whoever the saboteur is, it appears that he or she has won."

"Could we rebuild it ourselves?" Joe asked.

"I'm only allowed to use union labor, Joseph," Mr. Paul told him.

"We're already using Joe as a nonunion spot operator," Jennifer said. "To borrow the American phrase, I say we 'go for it.' Give me Frank, Joe, and Chris and we can have this rebuilt in a day or two."

"I couldn't. It's illegal," Mr. Paul said. "Even with free labor, we'd have to buy the lumber and hardware," Mr. Paul pointed out.

"What about the anonymous donation?" Frank asked.

"We need that for costumes," Mr. Paul replied.

"The school has quite a large costume collection," Chris suggested. "Perhaps we could borrow them."

"A production of this magnitude using worn-out, inexpensive school costumes?" Mr. Paul wondered aloud.

"It would be better than no production at all," Frank reasoned.

"Remember, Dad, the show must go on," Chris reminded him of the old saying.

"Everyone here would have to be willing to look the other way," Mr. Paul said, gesturing to the full cast and crew assembled. Everyone nodded or spoke their approval.

"Then it's settled," Chris said, smiling.

Jennifer made a list of all the materials she needed for the repairs and estimated the total cost. "I'll defer the cost of labor," she said, handing the list to Dennis Paul.

"Thank you, Jennifer," Mr. Paul said, then pulled out the bank envelope full of money.

"How did you get the money so quickly?" Chris asked.

"Oh, Mr. Kije happened to have it on hand in his office," Mr. Paul replied. "He exchanged it for the cashier's check."

Frank and Joe were stunned—Dennis Paul was lying.

Mr. Paul counted out fifteen hundred pounds and handed it to Chris.

"Take this to buy the lumber and other things," Mr. Paul instructed his son. "Meanwhile, I'll try to find Emily to calm her down."

"Do you have something I can put the money in?" Chris asked his father.

Mr. Paul opened his briefcase and found an open, used envelope.

Joe caught the name and address on the envelope: Kije Enterprises, Inc.

"Let me help you," Joe said, holding open the envelope while Mr. Paul transferred the money into it. Joe checked the address and silently repeated it until he had it memorized, then handed the envelope to Chris.

"Tell them we need the lumber delivered immediately," Dennis Paul told his son. "You and Joseph can carry back the other things yourselves."

"I'll stay with Jennifer and help clean up the mess," Frank offered.

"As will I," Mr. Paul added.

As Joe and Chris passed through the lobby, Joe noticed Corey Lista talking with Timothy Jeffries. "I'm sorry it had to come to this, Mr. Jeffries," Lista piped up loudly when he saw Joe. "But it's a matter of safety."

"Boys!" Jeffries called to Joe and Chris as they pushed open the theater doors. "What's going on now, where are you going?"

"To buy lumber to rebuild the set," Chris said, holding up the envelope.

"Well, excellent," Jeffries said after a hesitation. "Perhaps we'll open and be a hit after all."

As Joe and Chris trotted down the steps at the underground station, Joe asked his friend whether he had told anyone about the Haunted London tour.

"Sure," Chris replied, "a couple of my mates at school got a big laugh out of it."

"Did you tell your father?" Joe asked as he slipped his underground pass into the slot at the turnstile.

"Yeah. Why?" Chris asked, concern crossing his face.

Joe heard the rumble of a train approaching in the station and used it as an excuse to dodge Chris's question. "Let's hurry so we can catch this train."

"Hold this!" Chris said, handing Joe the envelope of money while he pulled his underground pass from his wallet.

After Chris went through the turnstile, the boys rushed down the steps and onto the crowded platform.

Joe saw the train pulling in at the far end of the station and stepped toward the edge of the platform. Suddenly someone grabbed the envelope in Joe's hand.

"Hey!" Joe shouted, hanging on to the envelope as the man, who looked like a punk rocker with long black hair and sunglasses, attempted to push Joe away and take it.

The envelope ripped wide open, scattering the money all over the platform. Joe was flung backward and over the edge of the platform, directly into the path of the oncoming train!

9 The Chase Down the Tube Tunnel

Joe heard the squeal of the train wheels as his shoulder struck the iron rail on the tracks.

"Joe!" Chris shouted, kneeling and stretching his hand down to the younger Hardy. Joe grabbed hold and jumped at the same time Chris yanked and was launched up onto the platform just as the front car of the train came to a stop at the spot where Joe had fallen.

Joe scanned the crowd, most of whom were staring at him. Then he spotted the thief pushing past people on the stairs.

Chris dropped to his hands and knees, collecting the money. "Forget about him, Joe, we have the money."

Joe Hardy's temper was up, and he pushed through the crowd, not heeding his friend. When he reached the top of the stairs, a yellow sign reading Way Out was to his right. To his left, signs pointed to Hammersmith and City, a different train line in the underground system.

Joe peered over a sea of pedestrians who made their way through the tunnel. Far away, he saw a head of long black hair duck down a staircase leading to the Hammersmith trains. Joe scuttled along the wall to the stairs, avoiding the swarm of people in the center of the tunnel.

When he reached the Hammersmith platform, it was dotted with a modest number of commuters. Joe feared a train had just left the station, carrying the thief with it. No one was moving toward the steps out, though, which confirmed for Joe that no train had just let off passengers. From behind a column at the far end of the platform, Joe saw a head of long black hair peek out.

Seeing Joe, the thief turned to run. Joe saw no stairs leading out at the thief's end of the platform and thought he had him cornered until the man dropped down onto the tracks and disappeared into the darkness of the subway tunnel.

Determined not to lose him, Joe climbed down onto the tracks and gave chase, disregarding the warning shouts of onlookers.

The tunnel was very dimly lit, but Joe pressed on, running down the tracks despite not being able to see the man he was pursuing. A light source around a bend ahead of him suddenly silhouetted the man, who had stopped dead.

The light source grew brighter, and Joe realized it was the lights of an oncoming train.

The man grabbed hold of a steel support beam and swiftly shimmied up it. Pushing aside a metal grate in the ceiling of the tunnel, he released himself from the support beam and hung over the tracks for a second before hoisting himself through the space in the grating.

Joe tried to follow, but the support beam offered no foot or handholds, and he slipped back down to the tracks. The Hammersmith train rounded the bend and Joe pressed his body against the wall behind the support beam.

The train whizzed by within a few inches of Joe's back, whipping his pant legs with the wind it created. After the train passed, Joe breathed a sigh of relief. He stared up at the grating through which the man had climbed and wondered about what sort of person had the strength and agility to make such an escape.

A flashlight beam suddenly shown in Joe's eyes. "All right, you. Move slowly toward me with your hands raised," the man holding the flashlight ordered.

As Joe stepped closer, he recognized the uniform of a transport officer.

A few minutes later Joe found himself with Chris in the office of the transport police, answering questions.

"You're telling me this geezer scaled the beam, pushed aside a fifty-pound grate, and climbed up to the street through the ventilation shaft?" the officer asked, wrinkling his forehead skeptically.

"He wasn't a geezer, he was a young man," Joe clarified.

"By 'geezer' he just means, oh, what would you Yanks say . . . a 'guy,' " Chris told him.

"You'd have to be a spider to reach the surface from that tunnel," the officer said.

"I don't know how he did it, either," Joe agreed.

"You should know better than to carry fifteen hundred quid around in an envelope," the officer scolded both of them. "London's full of pickpockets."

"This wasn't just a pickpocket," Joe told him, and briefly explained about the ghost of Quill Garden, the acts of sabotage in the theater, and the assailant they chased through the adjacent building during the walking tour of Haunted London.

"The Ghost of Quill Garden and Haunted London, eh?" the officer repeated. "You'd better stay away from Madame Tussaud's, or you'll be in here tomorrow telling me one of the wax works came to life and bit you."

"Joe's not irrational," Chris assured the man.

"He chased a pickpocket—who hadn't even gotten your money, I might add—into an active train tunnel," the officer pointed out. "The only blokes I know more irrational than that are dead ones."

"Sorry, I was angry," Joe replied, rubbing his shoulder where it had struck the iron rail of the tracks.

"I'm not making light of this, boys, but we get twenty complaints a day about cutpurses," the officer said earnestly. "I'll file this report right way."

"Thank you, officer," Joe said, rising.

* * *

Ninety minutes later Joe and Chris returned to the theater from the store and were busily helping Frank unload plywood off the back of a delivery truck in the side alley. The large trash bin overflowed with the damaged remains of the courthouse set, which Frank and Jennifer had cleared.

Chris went inside to help Jennifer measure and cut wood. While the Hardys continued unloading, they spoke privately about the recent events.

"Climbs like a spider?" Frank said thoughtfully. "Jennifer's pretty agile."

"What about Neville Shah?" Joe guessed.

Frank shook his head. "Not with a broken wrist."

"Maybe it's not really broken," Joe suggested.

"Jennifer told us that story. The whole crew saw Shah fall off the ladder," Frank reminded Joe. "And we've proven he couldn't have been the figure in white I saw in the lighting booth. He couldn't have reappeared on stage that quickly, even if he was Houdini."

"We're also sure that whoever is involved has an accomplice," Joe said.

"Not Emily Anderson, she was onstage," Frank recalled. "Jennifer was with me, and Mr. Paul was directing when the first 'accident' occurred."

"Mr. Jeffries claimed he was in his office at the time," Joe added.

"Couldn't be him, either. He came up the main staircase to the balcony," Frank said. "There's no way he could get from the back stairs to the main stairs without coming through the theater."

"Could there be more than one accomplice?" Joe pondered aloud.

"Possibly. If we could just track down Mr. Kije—" Frank began.

"One-eleven Old Castle Street, Suite five-oh-two," Joe blurted out, then explained about the address on the envelope that he had memorized.

"When we take a food break, you can check out Mr. Kije," Frank suggested. "Meanwhile, I'll talk to Emily Anderson's agent, Ian Link, see what I can find out about this other show she wants to do."

"Do you think he'll tell you anything?" Joe wondered.

"When I tell him I'm an intern working for Mr. Schulander, I think he might," Frank replied, smiling.

By late afternoon the Hardys and Chris had helped Jennifer rebuild the courthouse set piece, and put a base coat of white paint on it.

"The rest is detail and texturing to make the wood look like marble," Jennifer said.

"I've done quite a lot of that for school plays," Chris offered.

"Good, Chris, you stay with me," Jennifer said, then looked at the Hardys. "As much as I'd like to offer lessons, I think it'll be faster if Chris and I do it ourselves."

"Can't we help you attach the set piece to the pipe again?" Joe offered.

"Right, but we've got three hours of paint work to do

first," Jennifer replied. "So go out for a bite and be back at six."

Frank checked the London phone book and got the address for the Link Talent Agency. "Good luck, Joe. I'll see you back here at six o'clock," he said.

Joe rode on the top deck of a double-decker bus down Whitechapel Road, which became Aldgate High Street. He passed by numerous shops, pubs, and churches, getting off the bus at Commercial Street and walking up to Old Castle Street.

Joe scratched his head. One-eleven Old Castle Street wasn't an office building at all, but a narrow, somewhat dilapidated five-story tenement.

Inside, Joe walked up five flights of stairs and found a door marked 502. From the outside, Joe guessed he would not find a luxury office suite on the other side. He noticed a note pinned to the door: "Kije Enterprises Closed. Call For Appointment."

Joe copied down the phone number on the notice and used a pay phone outside to call.

"You have reached Kije Enterprises, Incorporated," a man with a foreign accent began on a recorded message. "Please leave your name, number, and the nature of your business at the tone and we shall return your call at our earliest opportunity."

"My business?" Joe said quietly to himself. "My business is to find out if you know Dennis Paul has cashed a three-thousand-pound check of yours—"

Just then Joe heard the tone. "Hi, this is Joe Hardy, I'm

a friend of Dennis Paul's. I need to talk to Mr. Kije about some troubling things happening with the show *Innocent Victim.*" Joe realized that the only number he could leave was Mr. Paul's or the one at the theater. He couldn't risk having Mr. Paul or anyone else at the theater know what he was up to, so he added, "Um, I'll try calling back."

Ian Link's receptionist greeted Frank rather coolly. "Yes, young man, what are you here for?"

"I wanted to see Mr. Link," Frank replied.

"Mr. Link isn't accepting new clients, and, no, you may not leave your photo and résumé," the receptionist snipped.

"I'm not an actor," Frank replied. "I work for Mr. Schulander."

"Oh, well, that's where Ian is," the receptionist replied, lightening her tone.

"Where?" Frank asked.

"At the Alhambra," she replied.

Frank was about to ask what the Alhambra was, then realized the question might blow his cover. "Thank you, I'll go to the Alhambra," Frank said instead.

As he stepped onto the elevator, a man in a sports coat was riding down to the lobby. "Excuse me, what is the Alhambra?" Frank asked.

The man smiled. "The Alhambra? It's one of the most prestigious theaters in the West End."

By the time he reached the ground floor, Frank had an address and directions and walked swiftly to London's West End.

As he walked through the front door of the Alhambra and started to enter the theater, an usher stopped him. "May I help you?"

"I need to see Ian Link," Frank replied.

"This is a closed audition, you'll have to wait for Mr. Link out here," the usher told him.

Frank wanted to get into that theater. He could not only talk to Ian Link, but possibly even Mr. Schulander himself. Remembering the stage door at the Quill Garden, he went around the side of the building. The Alhambra had a stage door, but there was a doorman guarding it.

After buying some coffee and a turkey sandwich at a nearby store, Frank returned to the stage door.

"I have an order for Mr. Schulander," he said to the man at the stage door.

"How'd you get your work visa?" the man asked.

Frank was thrown for a moment, then realized he was referring to Frank's being American. It was very difficult, he had heard, for Americans to get permission to work in England. "Connections" was all Frank replied.

The man let Frank in, and he followed the narrow corridor until he found the entrance to the stage. Through the main curtain, he heard a conversation going on in the front of the auditorium and stopped to listen.

"Ian, I would have loved for Emily to do the role," a man with a deep voice said, "but I find it wholly unethical to pull her from a show to which she's already committed."

"I'm telling you, Mr. Schulander, *Innocent Victim* is as good as dead before it even opens," the other man, who Frank assumed was Ian Link, replied. "Hold off casting for just another few days."

Suddenly someone grabbed Frank's shoulder and spun him around. "What do you think you're doing?" the man demanded.

Frank dropped the sandwich, stunned to be face-to-face with Corey Lista.

10 The Turncoat

"Come on, you," Lista said, pushing Frank through the curtain and out onto the lip of the stage.

"What's happening here?" Schulander asked, standing in the first row of seats with Ian Link.

"This one here sneaked in through the stage door," Lista said, grabbing Frank by the arm.

"What do you mean sneaking in, young man?" Schulander asked.

"I'm protecting the interests of Mr. Kije," Frank replied, pulling away from Lista's grasp. "I had a hunch you were trying to hire away the star of his show."

"I told Ian from the beginning that I had no intention of hiring away Emily," Schulander said, defending himself.

"But what if *Innocent Victim* gets scrapped?" Ian Link asked.

"That's another matter," Schulander replied. "But Timothy Jeffries is an old friend. For his sake, I hope it's a huge hit. I know how desperately he needs one at his theater."

"If you're a friend, why would you hire a stage manager who just quit the show in Mr. Jeffries theater?" Frank asked, nodding toward Lista.

"Mr. Lista was recommended to me by Mr. Jeffries himself just last night," Schulander replied.

"I had every right to quit," Lista snarled. "I explained the unsafe working conditions to my union, and they gave me their blessing."

"You're telling me you quit this morning and walked into another job this afternoon?" Frank challenged.

"I saw the writing on the wall, so I had been making inquiries," Lista replied. "Mr. Jeffries was nice enough to put in a good word."

"Well, young man, I wish you the best of luck with your show," Schulander said, escorting Frank to the stage door. "Now, if you would be so good as to let me attend to mine."

Frank and Joe met up outside the Quill Garden Theatre just as a light snow was beginning to fall. Joe filled in Frank on Kije Enterprises location in a shoddy apartment building, and the peculiar note hung on the door. Frank then told Joe about his encounter at the Alhambra Theatre.

"Schulander said Jeffries recommended Lista for the job *last night*," Frank told his brother.

"Why would Jeffries recommend Lista for another job before he had quit his job on *Innocent Victim?*" Joe wondered as they walked into the theater to get warm.

"Good question. And you were right about Emily Anderson. She was hoping *Innocent Victim* was canceled," Frank told him as they walked down the aisle toward the stage.

"Hoping it would be canceled and trying to cancel it are two different things," Emily Anderson said as she stepped from the wings onto the stage. "Yes, I heard you. You might recall, the acoustics in here are excellent."

Mr. Paul walked in from the wings behind Emily. "Good news, boys! Emily is still with us. She even apologized for her negative attitude."

Emily gave Mr. Paul an astonished look.

"Well, it wasn't exactly an apology," Mr. Paul conceded.

"I still have no interest in ending my career, or my life, because I get caught in the crossfire of whatever insidious plot is being perpetrated here," Emily said, walking off toward the dressing rooms. "One more incident, or for that matter, one more accusation," she added to the Hardys, "and I will break my contract and leave this show whether you sue me or not."

After Emily left, Joe asked, "Where are Jennifer and Chris?"

"Gone after more materials," Mr. Paul told them.

"Apparently, the counterweight system was damaged as well. Repairs will take all night, Jennifer thinks."

"We'll be glad to stay and help," Frank offered. "Tomorrow's Saturday, so we don't have to wake up early for school."

"That would be marvelous, boys. Then I can go to the school this evening and arrange to borrow the costumes," Mr. Paul replied, taking out his key chain. "Here are my keys. Be sure to lock up when you leave."

Mr. Paul buttoned up his overcoat, bid the Hardys' good night, and left.

"What do we know about repairing counterweight systems?" Joe wondered.

"The show is still going on, Joe," Frank told him. "I figure whoever is trying to sabotage *Innocent Victim* might try again tonight."

"And if they do, we'll be here," Joe finished Frank's thought.

Frank hopped up in the judge's high-backed swivel chair on the set and looked out at the hundreds of empty seats in the theater. It was a powerful feeling.

"Emily Anderson is the only one we've got with a motive," Joe said, sitting on the edge of the stage with his legs dangling down, "but I'm convinced she's telling the truth."

"Don't forget what a good actress she is," Frank reminded his younger brother. "Besides, if she isn't involved, who's been trying to frame her for the sabotage?"

"Someone who knew she used greasepaint and lit a red candle in her dressing room," Joe replied.

"One of the other actors?" Frank guessed. "But why choose to frame a woman with such an impeccable reputation? What motive—"

"Motive. That's it," Joe interrupted. "Emily Anderson had a motive that could make her a legitimate suspect. Maybe the real saboteur knew that."

Frank spun toward Joe in the judge's chair, "So he chose her to keep anyone investigating from digging for other suspects with other motives."

"Good hypothesis, Frank," Joe exclaimed, "but we still have no idea *who* we're talking about."

"There they are, the shirkers!" Chris called as he trudged down the aisle from the back of the theater, coils of rope and cable slung over his shoulder. Jennifer followed, carrying bags.

They were delighted to find that Frank and Joe would be working with them through the night.

"There's a new Indian restaurant that opened around the corner—we can order take-away," Jennifer suggested. "They have terrific goat curry and tandoori, not to mention the raita, the biryani, the naan, and the mango chutney."

"Naan, mango, tandoori, and goat?" Joe repeated. "Whatever you say. Sounds like a nice change from burgers and fries."

By two-thirty in the morning, the repairs to the counterweight system were complete. Joe stepped into the side alley to get a breath of fresh air and was surprised to find a foot of snow on the ground with the temperature still dropping.

Frank stepped outside, thumping his chest with his hand as he burped. "Excuse me. That Indian food was spicy."

"I thought it was excellent," Joe said, patting his stomach.

"The way you scarfed it down, you did a pretty good impression of our buddy Chet Morton," Frank said.

"Hey, we both have cast-iron stomachs," Joe said.

"Yeah, but in two different sizes," Frank said, grinning. "Medium and extra large."

The Hardys laughed together just as Chris and Jennifer stepped outside.

"It's good to hear you laughing," Chris said. "With all that's been going on, we haven't had much time to have fun."

"The fun can come later. Right now, the play's the thing," Joe told him.

"My goodness, Joe Hardy quoting Shakespeare?" Chris exclaimed in mock astonishment.

"I did?" Joe asked.

"Speaking of no fun, with this snow it'll be no fun getting home," Chris said. "Our train stopped running at midnight. We'll have to take a bus and then walk the rest."

"We have a nine o'clock call tomorrow morning. Why don't we all just sleep here?" Jennifer suggested.

Frank, Joe, and Chris agreed. After foraging backstage, they created makeshift beds from set furniture and covered themselves with black masking curtains for blankets.

"I'm glad Jennifer suggested this," Joe said privately to Frank, after they had bedded down on two sofas.

"Yeah, well, I kind of figured you liked being around her," Frank said, smiling.

"No, not that," Joe said, blushing slightly. "I'm glad because she wouldn't have suggested we stay here all night if she was one of the saboteurs."

"You're right, Joe," Frank said.

"Hey, you under the tormentor, keep it quiet," Chris joked to the Hardys from the chaise longue he was lying on.

"Tormentor?" Joe asked.

"That's the type of curtain you're using for a blanket," Chris replied. "Tormentors are hung on the sides of the stage behind the proscenium to block the audience's view of the wings. See, you learn something new from me every day."

All four of them chuckled a bit.

"Good night, gentlemen," Jennifer called from the other side of the stage, where she was lying on an army cot she had found in the storage area. "You did fine work."

"Should I turn off this light?" Joe asked, pointing to the one bare bulb on the stand in the middle of the stage."

"That's the work light," Jennifer told them. "You

leave it onstage when everyone leaves the theater so that the stage is never dark."

"Why?" Joe asked.

"Superstition," Jennifer said.

With that, they settled down to sleep.

When Frank's eyes opened, the stage was dark and his breath was frosty.

Joe still slept, curled up on his sofa.

"Joe!" Frank called in a hushed tone.

Joe's eyes blinked open. "Man, it's freezing in here," Joe said, sitting up and grabbing his heavy leather jacket.

"The power must have cut off," Frank said, feeling for his own jacket and putting it on before walking over to the chaise longue and shaking Chris awake.

"Don't tell me it's morning," Chris said, groggily.

"It's about five A.M.," Frank replied after hitting the light button on his watch and checking the time.

Joe walked over to wake Jennifer, but found her cot empty. He suddenly heard a faint, metallic clatter from high above him.

"I think someone's up on the catwalk above the stage," Joe whispered. "Jennifer?"

There was no answer, and the sound stopped.

Chris had now gotten up and was flipping light switches in the left wing. "No lights, either."

"Where's the breaker switch?" Joe asked.

"I have no idea," Chris replied. "We might find flashlights in the light booth or in Mr. Jeffries's office."

"You two go ahead, I'll keep looking for Jennifer," Joe said.

While Frank and Chris felt along the wall, moving up the side aisle toward the lobby of the theater, Joe started toward the dressing rooms.

Suddenly Joe heard another sound from high above the stage. A creak, like rusty hinges being forced open. Finding his way to the ladder, he began climbing up into the darkness toward the catwalk.

In the light booth, Frank found a flashlight. "Let's get down to the lobby to see if we can locate the breaker box," Frank told Chris.

"Frank! Chris!" Joe's voice echoed from somewhere nearby.

"Sounds like something's wrong," Frank said, and hurried in the direction of his brother's voice.

Up on the catwalk, Joe Hardy squinted, looking at something thin and gray, floating in the darkness. Lights suddenly came on below, illuminating the catwalk enough for Joe to see he was looking at gray light from outside, showing through a crack in the side wall of the stage house.

"Joe?" Frank's voice called from far below.

"I'm up here!" Joe called back.

Crossing to the end of the catwalk, Joe discovered the light was not coming through a crack, but through a small, rusty metal door that had been left ajar.

Joe pushed the door open, stepped out, and found himself on the snow-covered roof of the theater.

New footprints in the snow led toward the edge of the roof where Jennifer Mulhall stood staring down.

Joe moved toward the edge of the roof. "Jennifer?" Joe called quietly, not wanting to frighten her.

Jennifer turned to Joe, then shouted, "Watch out! He's right behind you!"

11 Hanging by a Thread

A violent shove from behind sent Joe Hardy stumbling forward and over the three-foot retaining wall that bordered the roof.

Joe grabbed hold of the storm gutter, which tore away from the outer wall of the building under his weight.

Joe was left dangling six stories above the street, hanging on to the aluminum gutter, one end of which remained uncertainly fastened to the outer wall by an iron brace.

He tried to get a foothold on the wall, but the gutter had left him hanging too far away to reach.

"Here!" Jennifer shouted, hanging over the retaining wall while rapidly feeding the metal tape from a tape measure down to Joe.

Joe grabbed the tape with one hand and wrapped it around his wrist. The edge of the metal tape cut into Joe's palm as Jennifer began hoisting him up.

"Joe?" Jennifer cried out.

She had wrapped the other end of the tape around her own hand to keep it from detaching from the casing, and it was cutting into her skin.

Joe knew she couldn't hang on for more than a few seconds, but he could not climb up without letting go of the gutter. His full weight would either break the tape or pull Jennifer off the roof.

Joe looked down, but there was no ledge below to which he could jump. A set of hands suddenly grasped him by the shoulders of his leather jacket.

Frank hung far over the retaining wall, supported by Chris. Together, all three of them were able to hoist Joe up and over the wall and back on to the roof.

As the four of them sat, breathless, Jennifer explained that she hadn't seen the face of Joe's attacker because his head was lowered and then her attention was focused on helping Joe. She did say the man was tall with dark hair. Frank asked her to go back to the beginning and tell what had happened.

"I heard something up on the catwalk," she began. "I thought perhaps it was only mice or a rat, so I didn't want to disturb your sleep."

"Only mice or a rat, so you didn't want to disturb us?" Chris repeated, panting. "Jennifer, you would never fall into the category of shrinking violet."

"Thank you," she replied.

"I heard something, too," Joe told her, as he and the others got to their feet.

"You probably heard me," Jennifer said. "I found the old service door to the roof open."

"It's usually locked?" Frank asked.

"With a padlock, which I've never seen off it until tonight," Jennifer replied. "Footprints led to the edge of the roof, then disappeared. Whoever it was, I thought he had escaped."

Joe had been surveying the roof. "He must have been hiding on the water tower," Joe said, pointing to the elevated tank behind them.

"Still, how did he get off the roof?" Chris wondered.

"Which footprints were the ones you initially saw, Jennifer?" Frank asked.

Jennifer pointed them out.

"You can see your tracks and Joe's are pointing toward the edge of the roof," Frank said. "The other tracks are pointing toward the door to the catwalk."

"You're right, Frank!" Jennifer exclaimed. "I hadn't looked closely until now."

"And this person's tracks already have quite a bit of new fallen snow in them," Frank added.

"Meaning?" Chris asked.

"Meaning that our mystery man or woman got into the theater from the roof," Joe told him, following Frank's train of thought.

"But the lock to the roof door had been removed from the inside," Jennifer pointed out.

"Perhaps an accomplice who's involved with *Innocent*

Victim left the door unlocked for the saboteur," Chris suggested.

"But how did this person get onto the roof in the first place?" Jennifer wondered.

"Here's a fresh set of the same footprints leading from the place where I was pushed to the edge of the roof," Joe said, following them and then kneeling beside a long depression in the snow. "Looks like he picked something up that was lying here."

Frank noticed the shape: an oblong rectangle about ten feet long and one foot wide. He then looked across the alley to the roof of the abandoned building, which was nearly parallel in height to the theater roof.

"A plank!" Frank exclaimed as the thought struck him.

Getting a hunch, Joe ran to the side of the roof facing the back alley and looked down. He saw a figure running out the rear door of the abandoned building. As the figure passed beneath a streetlight, Joe recognized the wild black hair of the man who had tried to rob him in the underground.

"Let's go!" Joe shouted, leading the group back through the roof door, across the catwalk, and down the ladder.

"Jennifer, you phone the police," Frank shouted as he, Joe, and Chris ran through the lobby.

The boys crashed out the door of the theater and ran to the back of the abandoned building. There they followed the tracks in the snow that led away from the rear door.

"We're lucky," Joe said as they ran. "This early in the morning, there won't be many other tracks to confuse us."

Joe was right. The group followed the mystery man's tracks for several blocks with ease. Then they reached a major intersection where early morning foot traffic had left prints all over the sidewalk.

"There he is!" Joe exclaimed in a hushed voice, spotting the man with black hair crossing the street two blocks down.

Frank and the others took off running, staying on their side of the street, hoping that the man wouldn't spot them. They were nearly adjacent to him when the man glanced over his shoulder.

Seeing the Hardys, he took off running. Frank, Joe, and Chris pursued the man at a sprint for nearly a quarter mile through the streets of London. Chris was not as athletic as the Hardys and lagged behind, so Joe slowed to keep pace with him while Frank moved ahead.

Looming in front of them was the great dome of St. Paul's Cathedral.

When the man reached the gigantic structure, he bounded up the great stone steps and into the cathedral with Frank only fifty yards behind.

When Chris and Joe reached the main entrance, a security guard stopped them.

"St. Paul's isn't open to visitors for another two hours," he told them.

"We're chasing a man who tried to push me off a roof," Joe said, huffing and puffing.

"His brother followed the man in here not fifteen seconds ago!" Chris added, hands on his knees, trying to catch his breath.

Joe scanned the main chamber of the cathedral, which stretched for blocks in front of him. A cleaning crew was polishing the floor, but he didn't see Frank or the man with long black hair.

"If they got past me, they must have veered off into one of the galleries," the guard said, pointing to both sides, beyond the giant support pillars that lined the main seating area of the cathedral.

Joe and Chris split up and moved to separate sides of the cathedral.

Joe rounded one of the pillars just in time to see Frank disappearing into an alcove across from the central dome.

As Frank bounded up the stairs in the alcove, he passed a sign pointing up to the Whispering Gallery. Two hundred and fifty steps later, he reached it. The Whispering Gallery circled around the base of the great dome.

Frank wondered why it was called the Whispering Gallery. As he paused, catching his breath, he found out. He heard footsteps nearby, but then saw the man with the black hair across the dome on the other side of the gallery, a hundred feet away. The footsteps he heard were his!

The man held something to his ear and spoke in a hushed voice. Frank held his breath and listened.

"I'm at St. Paul's, the Americans followed me," the man said with a foreign accent. Frank realized he was speaking into a cellular phone. "If I'm caught, you can forget about the corner kick."

Frank listened, stunned that he could understand the man speaking a hundred feet away as if he were right beside him. His throat felt raw from his long run in the bitter cold, and he tried to suppress a cough, but couldn't.

The man heard him, and ran up another set of stairs on the other side of the Whispering Gallery. Frank followed, winding up a steep, spiral staircase that led to the Stone Gallery.

As Frank reached the top of the staircase, he found himself looking out at a grand vista of London. The Stone Gallery ran around the outside of the great dome. Frank rounded the entire gallery and found yet another staircase that led up to the Golden Gallery at the pinnacle of the dome.

Frank had his foot on the first step before he stopped, realizing that the man would be trapping himself by going to the top of the dome.

Rushing to the high railing that surrounded the Stone Gallery, he looked down and spotted the man climbing down one of the huge stone pillars, using some kind of suction devices to cling to the smooth surface.

"Frank!" Joe called as he ran to his brother's side. "Where is he?"

Frank frowned and pointed down.

"This guy's not human!" Joe exclaimed.

"Hurry!" Frank shouted, pointing back to the stairs leading down.

They reached the Whispering Gallery and hurried out to the pillar, but there was no sign of the man who had climbed down it.

"Do you think he fell?" Joe wondered, looking down.

A commotion erupted below them. Running back into the Whispering Gallery, they looked down to the main floor of the cathedral, where the man with black hair pushed aside the security guard and headed for the entrance.

"He suckered us into following him up here," Frank realized. "Where's Chris?"

"He couldn't keep up, I left him downstairs!" Joe recalled.

Frank spotted their friend near the entrance. "Chris!" he shouted, his voice echoing through the cathedral.

Chris looked up, and Frank and Joe pointed frantically to the fleeing suspect.

"Go after him!" Frank shouted.

Chris took off, reaching the entrance to the cathedral only a second after the suspect had run out.

By the time the Hardys reached the street outside St. Paul's, Chris and the man were nowhere to be seen.

"They went west and turned on Maria Lane," the security guard called to them from the steps of the cathedral.

Following the security guard's directions, the Hardys ran into Chris a few blocks up Maria Lane.

"Another disappearing act," Chris said, and motioned for them to follow.

The Hardys followed Chris to a small courtyard behind three apartment buildings.

"An apparent dead end," Chris explained, "but when I turned the corner not fifteen seconds behind this geezer, he was gone."

The fire escape ladder on one building hung about ten feet off the ground. Joe walked up beneath it. "Our guy could climb the wall to this fire escape, no problem," Joe commented.

"Looks like you're right, Joe," Frank said, picking up a long black wig that had been tossed behind a nearby trash bin.

"Do you think he climbed to the roof?" Joe asked.

Frank shook his head. "Five stories up? Chris would have spotted him before he reached the top. I think he went through the window of one of these apartments."

"Let's go talk to the super," Joe suggested.

"The super?" Chris asked, puzzled, then realized. "Oh, the property manager!"

The boys walked around the block to the front of the building. Frank was about to buzz the doorbell of the apartment labeled Manager when Joe suddenly grabbed his arm and pointed up. "Look, Frank!"

Over the front entrance etched in the stone was the building's address: 117 Hayworth.

"One-seventeen Hayworth," Frank said aloud, thinking. Then he exclaimed, "That's Neville Shah's address!"

12 The Human Spider

Joe scanned the names of the tenants next to the door buzzers. "Shah, apartment number three-B. We don't need to talk to the building super, Frank, we need to call Detective Inspector Ryan."

Thirty minutes later Detective Inspector Ryan had the property manager let them into Neville Shah's second floor apartment.

Frank moved to an open window and looked out onto the back courtyard, but Neville Shah had disappeared again.

Joe noticed three identical framed posters depicting ornamented and costumed elephants. The posters were written in three different languages.

"Circus posters," Joe said, looking closely at the lettering. "From America, France, and India, I think." He spotted the picture of a spider in the top corner of each poster and read aloud the legend below the one printed in English: "'Witness the astounding feats of Anacro, the Human Spider.'"

"Do you think Neville Shah is Anacro?" Frank asked.

"Either that or he really loved this circus," Joe remarked.

"Mr. Shah had yet another profession," Detective Inspector Ryan said, pulling a computer printout from his jacket pocket. "He served a five-year sentence for burglarizing luxury high rises in Chicago. I ran a check on the name before I left Scotland Yard."

"But how could he do all that climbing with a broken wrist?" Chris wondered.

"Like this," Joe said, pulling the wrist cast Shah had been wearing from beneath his bed.

"Do you mean that whole fall from the ladder last week was staged?" Chris asked.

"That's my guess," Joe said.

"Fine work, boys," Detective Inspector Ryan said. "Looks like we have our man."

"Our man," Frank agreed, "but not our motive. Why would Shah break into the Quill Garden Theatre just to sabotage *Innocent Victim*?"

"I'll take the investigation from here," Detective Inspector Ryan said. "I might have more questions for you later."

"We'll be at the theater," Chris told him.

* * *

Bleary eyed and weary, the boys found a café just opening its doors for breakfast. Frank ordered kippers with a side of bubble and squeak.

"What's kippers and bubble and squeak?" Joe wondered.

Frank shrugged and looked at Chris.

"You'll find out when it gets here," his English friend said, smiling.

"I've had enough adventures for one day," Joe said, smiling to the waitress. "I'll have scrambled eggs and bacon."

"What would make Neville Shah resort to this?" Chris wondered.

"He was a burglar, so we know that he used to commit crimes to make big money," Joe pointed out.

"I heard Shah talking on a cellular phone in the cathedral," Frank told them. "He said, 'If I'm caught, you can forget about the corner kick.' What could that mean?"

Joe shook his head. "You got me."

"Corner kick is a football term," Chris said, adding to Joe, "Sorry, I mean a *soccer* term."

Joe sat straight up as a thought occurred to him. "The man on Kije Enterprises' answering machine had an accent like Neville's," Joe said. "Do you think you could identify Neville's voice, Chris?"

"I suppose," Chris replied.

"Kije," Frank muttered.

"What?" Joe asked.

"Nothing, go ahead," Frank said, reaching into his jacket pocket and pulling out a cassette tape.

Joe and Chris walked to the rear of the café and found a pay phone. After dialing, Joe handed the receiver to Chris. He saw a look of distress cross Chris's face as he listened to Kije Enterprises' recorded announcement.

"So what do you think?" Joe asked.

"What? No, it's not Neville," Chris said, seeming suddenly preoccupied. "Let's eat our breakfast."

When they returned to the table, breakfast had been served. Frank was focused on the liner notes from the cassette tape he had borrowed from Mr. Paul.

"Looks like bubble and squeak is potatoes and cabbage," Joe said, grinning over Frank's mystery breakfast. "And kippers are little smoked fish."

"I'm more interested in this," Frank told him. "The 'Lieutenant Kije Suite' is a piece of classical music written by Prokofiev for an old movie."

"That's an odd bit of coincidence, but so what?" Chris said, pushing his food around on the plate but not eating.

"Listen," Frank said, referencing the liner notes from the cassette tape. "In the movie, Lieutenant Kije was the name of an officer the other soldiers used as a scapegoat whenever they got into trouble. But in truth, Kije didn't exist."

"I still don't see—" Chris began.

"Kije could be an alias," Frank jumped in. "And your dad is the one who gave me this tape."

"Are you accusing my father of something?" Chris asked. "Why aren't we investigating Jennifer Mulhall?"

"Jennifer was with us," Joe reminded him.

"But Shah must have an accomplice," Chris countered. "Don't you find her story odd? She hears ruddy rats crawling about and doesn't wake us up?"

"I believe her," Joe said.

"The lock on that roof door had to be unlocked from the inside, Joe," Chris reminded him.

"And anyone with keys, including Mr. Jeffries or your father, could have unlocked it," Joe replied.

"We're the first renters Jeffries has had in over a year—why would he undermine the show?" Chris said. "And as for my father, he wrote and directed it."

"And he's ripping off the producer!" Joe exclaimed, his temper and exhaustion getting the best of him.

"We don't know that for sure, Chris, but he looks suspicious," Frank said, and explained to Chris about what had happened at the bank with the cashier's check.

"The money the anonymous donor gave to Mr. Kije went right into your dad's pocket," Joe added.

Chris looked dumbstruck. "The anonymous donor," he said, "was me."

"You?" Joe asked.

"Three thousand pounds. My whole savings account," Chris told them.

"Is that where you went the day you left us in the Lamb and Wolf Pub?" Joe asked. "To the bank to take out the money?"

Chris nodded. "Yes. And I'm afraid you may be right

about my dad. That voice on the answering machine for Kije Enterprises is his."

"What about the accent?" Frank asked.

"My dad's a theater teacher, he can do all sorts of dialects," Chris said. "That was Dad doing East Indian."

"But why would he set up a dummy company like Kije Enterprises?" Joe asked.

Chris shook his head. "I don't know."

Outside the Quill Garden Theatre, the boys were surprised to find all was quiet. Frank wondered if the police had already come, talked to Jennifer, and left.

While Frank used Mr. Paul's keys to open the front door, Joe went in through the back door of the adjacent building to check the roof.

Sure enough, he found foot prints in the snow there, too. Hidden under the debris on the roof, he discovered a twelve-foot wooden plank. He was certain now how the Human Spider had been getting into the theater unnoticed, but he still didn't know why.

Inside the theater, Joe found Frank standing alone on the stage.

"Now that we know Shah was involved, we're blowing all kinds of holes in the ghost theory," Frank told him. "By coming in through the door on the roof, he could have pulled the screws out of the courthouse facade and sabotaged the lights with greasepaint without anyone seeing him."

"What about the fire in Emily's dressing room?" Joe asked.

113

"Remember, we couldn't figure out how someone got past you and Chris?" Frank reminded him.

"Yeah." Joe answered.

Chris suddenly popped up from beneath the stage through a trapdoor. "Like many stages, this one has a trapdoor," Chris said. "There's a crawl space beneath the stage, leads to the stage right wing."

"So then Shah could have lit that fire and evaded Chris and me without being a ghost," Joe realized.

Frank nodded. "The crawl space is almost directly under the stage right door. Shah could have ducked into it just as you and Chris came through the door. Then he could have come up through the trapdoor, climbed to the catwalk, and gone out over the roof."

"That's why the emergency exit siren wasn't triggered," Chris added.

Joe snapped his fingers as he figured out another piece of the puzzle. "Shah also had to be the person who stole the tour guide's costume and tried to push the gate on top of you, Frank," Joe guessed.

"But how did he escape from the roof of the abandoned building?" Frank wondered.

"The same way he always got from that roof into the theater," Joe replied. "He walked the plank."

"But how did Shah know to find us at the Seven Bells Pub?" Frank asked.

Joe shook his head. "And who was the white figure you saw in the lighting booth?"

"More unanswered questions," Frank remarked.

"Speaking of questions, where's Jennifer?" Joe asked.

"I rang her flat," Chris said, "but no one answered."

"Aren't you a little concerned?" Joe pressed on. "The last thing we told her to do was phone the police. The police aren't here, Mr. Paul's not here, no one's here."

"Maybe she left a note," Frank said.

While Joe and Chris checked the lobby, Frank checked the lighting booth. Frank found no note, but sensed something in the booth was different. The computerized lighting board was gone!

Rushing downstairs, Frank found Joe and Chris outside the theater talking with Mr. Paul.

"Hello, Frank," Mr. Paul said. "The boys were telling me the disturbing news."

"Hadn't you heard already?" Frank asked.

"He hasn't heard from Jennifer or the police," Joe told him.

"I have more bad news," Frank told them. "Someone stole the light board."

"Neville Shah?" Chris wondered.

"No, Neville Shah wasn't carrying anything when we chased him," Joe said.

"He must have had an accomplice," Frank said, looking at Dennis Paul, then at Chris.

"Dad, we need to discuss something," Chris told his father. Chris confessed to being the anonymous donor and told his father everything they knew about Mr. Kije.

"Oh, Chris, you shouldn't have used your money," Mr. Paul scolded.

"Never mind about my money, Dad," Chris said. "I want to know about Kije Enterprises."

"I'm sorry, boys, I should have come out with it as soon as the trouble started," Mr. Paul said, then sighed heavily. "I am Mr. Kije."

13 Mr. Kije Appears

"What do you mean?" Chris asked.

"When my uncle Jared died last year, he left me a large sum of money, requesting that I use it to produce *Innocent Victim,*" Mr. Paul explained.

"Why?" Joe asked.

"My uncle knew how much I believed in my script and knew it was my dream to have it mounted onstage," Mr. Paul replied.

"But why didn't you just use your own name?" Chris wondered.

"Because it would be a vanity production," Frank guessed, remembering the conversation from a few days earlier. "Like Lord Quill's ill-fated production for his wife."

"Yes," Mr. Paul said. "Not only would it jeopardize its

chances for success with the critics to have my name on the show as producer, it was simply too embarrassing to have people think I was such an egomaniac. If I was producing and directing my own script, actors like Emily Anderson would have found it amateurish. She might not even have accepted her role."

"But it's a wonderful show, Mr. Paul," Frank said. "You shouldn't be embarrassed."

"Yes, well, my behavior has been foolhardy," Mr. Paul admitted. "But I assure you I have done nothing to undermine my play. When I told you I was meeting with Mr. Kije, I was actually visiting every show business investor I knew, trying to raise additional money."

"The private investigator told us you had gone to several homes that night," Joe recalled.

"Private investigator?" Chris and Dennis Paul chorused.

Joe explained about Mr. Jeffries hiring a private investigator to investigate the incidents at the theater.

"Well, whoever else is behind this, I'm afraid they've finally done us in," Mr. Paul said. "We've lost two days of rehearsal and we can't do a show without a light board."

By ten-thirty A.M., the police had once again come and gone. When Jeffries arrived, Mr. Paul told him about the events of the preceding night, even going so far as to admit his deception about Kije Enterprises.

"Mr. Paul, I have been extremely lenient," Jeffries began. "I have looked the other way while you allowed

118

nonunion labor—teenagers, in fact—to run your spot-lights and rebuild your sets."

"Yes, you've been very kind," Mr. Paul replied.

"I forgave the fact that you nearly burned down my theater," Jeffries went on. "I might even have forgiven you misrepresenting yourself to me as Mr. Kije. But now my state-of-the-art, computerized light board has been stolen by someone on your staff."

"We told you, it was Neville Shah," Joe protested.

"Detective Inspector Ryan has informed me that Mr. Shah is a possible suspect, based mainly on your testi-mony and a wig of some sort," Jeffries said, dismissively. "In any case, according to our contract, you are respon-sible for any of the theater's equipment, including the light board, which you use for your production."

"Yes, well, I'm certain it will turn up," Mr. Paul said.

"It will cost ten thousand pounds to replace it," Jef-fries told him. "I would like it by tomorrow morning."

"You're well aware that I don't have ten thousand pounds," Mr. Paul said coolly.

"Yes. I am also well aware that I am out of patience, so I'm willing to cut my loses," Jeffries said. "Now, I could simply toss you out for breach of contract, but since I have some sense of pity, I will allow you to sign a new agreement, releasing each of us from our obliga-tion to each other."

"That is generous, but I—" Mr. Paul began to say.

"Your advance rent will cover the cost of replacing the light board," Jeffries said, then turned and walked off. Frank watched him retreat into his office.

"What possible benefit could there be for Mr. Jeffries not allowing *Innocent Victim* to go on?" Frank asked Dennis Paul.

"None I can think of," Mr. Paul replied. "Up until now, he's been threatening to sue me if *I* broke our rental agreement. Now, he appears to want the contract broken."

"Hmm," Frank said, scratching the back of his neck thoughtfully. "What could you do to Mr. Jeffries if *he* broke the contract?"

"Well, I could sue him in return," Mr. Paul replied.

"Just for the money you had already given him?" Frank wondered.

"No, if his breach of contract brought about the demise of the show, I could sue him for all my costs, which is the entire budget of *Innocent Victim*. I could even sue for its potential earnings," Mr. Paul said.

"For hundreds of thousands," Joe concluded.

"I suppose, but not in this case," Mr. Paul said. "Jeffries has grounds to break the rental contract, given everything that's happened."

"Unless he's the cause of everything that's happened," Joe said

"But that's rather far-fetched, Joseph," Mr. Paul said. "Jeffries would have to have a lot to gain to take that sort of risk."

"So what do you want to do, Dad?" Chris asked.

"Go on with rehearsal," Mr. Paul replied. "I'll try to beg, borrow, or steal a light board somehow."

By noon rehearsal was in full swing. Emily Anderson

seemed inspired, Frank thought, and Chris took full command of the stage. The cast had pulled together as never before. It was sad to think it might all be over the next day.

Joe sat down next to Frank in the back row of the theater.

"Any luck finding Jennifer?" Frank asked.

"She's still not home and none of her neighbors have seen her," Joe replied quietly. "I'm worried."

Frank looked at his brother, trying to figure out how to broach a sensitive subject. "Joe, has it occurred to you that Jennifer might have been working *with* Neville Shah and has been fooling us all along? She may have disappeared because she stole the light board herself."

"That could be true," Joe replied, frowning. "But I'm hoping it's not."

Joe heard a faint metallic tapping noise coming from somewhere in the theater. "What's that sound?"

"The heating system is probably ancient," Frank guessed. "It's the pipes in the walls, filling with steam."

Joe nodded, then asked, "Has Mr. Paul had any luck finding another light board?"

Frank shook his head. "It's not like a cup of sugar he can borrow from a neighbor," Frank said. The words were just out of his mouth when an idea struck him. "Or maybe it is."

Frank rose to his feet. "Hold down the fort, Joe, I'm going to try to borrow a cup of sugar."

Frank left the theater. Joe started to follow, wanting

121

more of an explanation, but stopped when he saw Timothy Jeffries leading a man in a business suit out of his office. The man, whom Joe felt he had seen before, stood with Jeffries at the back of the theater, watching the rehearsal.

Jeffries was pointing to one thing and then another. Joe crouched and slipped along the partition between the lobby and the theater to see if he could hear what was being said.

"It's a grand space," the man said.

"Yes, Mr. Blanco, with plenty of room for dancing," Jeffries added.

Dancing? Was this a producer planning to do a musical, Joe wondered?

"Dancing isn't a main feature," Blanco said. "It's mostly men."

"Yes, of course. Now, here is the inspection slip. The electrical system, you can see, is up to code," Jeffries told him.

Suddenly the two men rounded the corner into the lobby. Joe rose swiftly and walked directly toward them, so as not to look as if he was hiding. "Hello," he said politely.

"Hello, young man," Blanco said. "So sorry to hear your show won't be opening."

"Not opening? I think it'll be one of the biggest hits of the year. I give it two thumbs up!" Joe said, enthusiastically thrusting his two thumbs into the air.

Joe watched Jeffries's face turn crimson as he tried to hold his temper.

"I thought you said—" Blanco began to question Jeffries.

"The producer has broken several rules stipulated in our rental agreement," Jeffries assured him. "If they don't leave peaceably, I have the legal right to force them out."

"But what have they done?" Blanco asked.

"We can talk more about that later this afternoon," Jeffries said, pushing out a smile. "When there aren't feelings to be hurt."

Jeffries led Blanco to the front door.

"So, I'll trot off to the bank and be back," Blanco said to Jeffries.

Joe spotted a white limousine waiting at the curb. Like lightning, the memory of where he had seen Blanco shot into Joe's head. Blanco had been in the Lamb and Wolf Pub with John Moeller, the soccer star.

As Blanco slipped into the limo, Jeffries closed the theater door and strode angrily up to Joe.

"Stay out of my business," he demanded. "Do you understand?"

"The man asked me a question and I answered," Joe replied, undaunted. "Why are you showing the theater when you already have a show in it, Mr, Jeffries?"

"A show will *not* be in it if my state-of-the-art light board is not recovered," Jeffries said with a smug smile.

"My brother is taking care of that right now," Joe said confidently, trying to provoke a reaction.

"Well, well—" Jeffries stammered, clearly thrown. "Even so, the word in the theater community of London is that *Innocent Victim* is a troubled show. In layman's terms, that means it has disaster written all over it. So I am looking for new renters now, so that my theater doesn't stay dark for another year after Mr. Kije-Paul's show closes."

"Mr. Blanco is a theater producer?" Joe asked.

Again, Jeffries stumbled on his words. "He's, he's— yes!"

"What's the name of the musical?" Joe pressed on with the rapid questions.

"What musical?" Jeffries demanded.

"I heard you mention 'room for dancing' to him," Joe said.

"Yes, a musical," Jeffries sputtered. "A musical, I don't know the name."

From this short exchange, Joe now felt certain that Jeffries was hiding something and had some secret reason for wanting *Innocent Victim* out of his theater.

"Will you recommend Neville Shah again to do lights?" Joe asked the theater owner.

"Jennifer Mulhall knew he was an ex-convict as well," Jeffries insisted. "We wanted to help him. Ask her if you don't believe me."

"I would, but she's disappeared," Joe said, staring into Jeffries' eyes.

Jeffries drew himself up, smiled, and stepped forward, looking up at the taller Joe Hardy. "You're an exchange student. Why don't you just try to enjoy yourself so you can leave England next week with fond memories, instead of regrets."

Jeffries turned and walked back into his office. Despite Jeffries's smiling face, Joe knew he had been threatened.

"You have incredible nerve, I'll give you that," Schulander said to Frank Hardy, who stood across from the producer's desk in a posh executive suite, holding a bag containing a roast beef sandwich.

"I had to figure out some way to get by your receptionist," Frank said.

"Yes, not much of a ruse, bringing me roast beef when I'm a vegetarian," Schulander said.

"I guess your receptionist doesn't know your eating habits," Frank said, smiling.

"Yes, she's new. All right, so what do you want? A job, an audition?" Schulander asked.

"I want a light board," Frank replied, and explained the situation at the Quill Garden, including all the acts of sabotage that had been plaguing the production.

"I know that your good friend Mr. Jeffries would appreciate your help," Frank concluded with a statement he knew was a necessary lie.

"Let's not exaggerate," Schulander said. "Jeffries is an acquaintance of mine, as is every other theater owner in town."

Frank's shoulders drooped as he prepared for Schulander to send him away empty-handed.

"However, in this difficult business, we must all help each other whenever we can, else the theater shall die,"

Schulander said, rising and walking to a huge wall calender covered with handwritten notes.

"I have a show in Covent Garden closing tonight," Schulander continued. "However, all the lighting equipment, including the board, is rented through the end of the week. You may borrow it."

"Mr. Schulander, I don't know how to thank you," Frank said, grinning.

"You could begin by bringing me falafel next time," Schulander said. "Now let's arrange for you to pick up that equipment. After all . . ."

". . . the show must go on," Frank and Schulander said in unison.

Frank left the theater and headed down the steps into the Leicester Square tube station.

The bright sun had begun to melt the snow from the night before, and as Frank trotted out of the Aldgate East tube stop near the theater, he felt hopeful about the Pauls' new show.

As he started to cross the intersection, he hesitated, remembering to look right, instead of left, before crossing to the median halfway across.

But as he stepped into the street, Frank heard an engine race to his left. Turning his head, he saw a car driving in reverse headed straight for him.

14 A Forgotten Ally

The car slammed on its brakes and stopped a few yards before it reached Frank.

David Young stepped out of the car. "Hello, Frank," he said. "Get in."

Frank felt uncertain about this.

"We're a block from the theater, I don't want anyone to see us talking," Young explained.

Frank nodded and then got into Young's European compact car. Young looked like a giant crammed into the driver's seat of the tiny automobile as he drove Frank around the block.

"Mr. Young, what are you doing here?" Frank asked.

"I've been here for twenty-one hours now," Young told him, referring to a pile of empty cardboard coffee cups on the backseat of the car.

"Mr. Jeffries told you to stake out the theater?" Frank asked.

"Mr. Jeffries didn't much like my conclusion that you boys and Dennis Paul were innocent," Young told him. "When I said I planned to watch the theater overnight to see who the real culprit might be, he sacked me."

"Sacked you?" Frank asked.

"Fired me," Young replied. "So I figured I'd better stake it out for *your* sake, if you know what I mean."

"Then you saw us when we chased after Neville Shah," Frank realized.

"I didn't know who or what you were chasing," Young said.

"Where did Jennifer go?" Frank asked.

"Back into the theater," Young replied. "Then Jeffries came out about six A.M."

"Came out?" Frank repeated. "Don't you mean, went in?"

"Never saw him go in," Young answered. "Only saw him come out. Then again, I might have been dozing when he arrived."

"What about Jennifer?" Frank asked.

Young shook his head. "I didn't see her come out at all. You might want to ask Jeffries, since he was here."

"Thank you, Mr. Young," Frank said, getting out of the car and turning to shake Young's hand through the window. "You've helped us a lot."

"Well, I feel a bit of kinship to my American investigative counterparts," Young said with a smile. "So long for now," he added before driving off.

Frank hurried across the street and into the theater where he found the cast on a five-minute break. He told them all the good news about Schulander and the light board he was lending to them.

Joe pulled Frank aside and into the lobby. He related his news about Blanco and Jeffries' conversation and about Jeffries's veiled threat.

"Jeffries might also have something to do with Jennifer's disappearance," Frank said, and told him what he had learned from David Young. "Mr. Young saw Jennifer go into the theater after we left her, but she never came out. He saw Jeffries come out of the theater early this morning, but never saw him go in."

"Do you think he took her hostage?" Joe wondered.

Frank shrugged. "I don't see Jeffries taking a hostage up the ladder and over the roof, and he would have tripped the alarm if he went out the fire exit in back."

"Blanco and Jeffries are meeting again later this afternoon," Joe told Frank. "Listening in on that meeting might be our best chance to find out what Jeffries is up to."

Just then a man in a chauffeur's uniform walked into the theater and into Jeffries's office. The chauffeur reemerged with Jeffries a moment later.

"Here we go," Joe said quietly to Frank, stepping over to the front door after Jeffries had left.

Joe caught a glimpse of Blanco in the backseat as the chauffeur opened the rear door for Jeffries. As the limousine pulled away from the curb, Joe and Frank stepped outside and the younger Hardy flagged down a taxi.

"Follow that white limousine," Frank told the driver as he got into the back of the taxi with Joe.

The limousine stopped briefly in front of a storefront with the name Union Fidelity Title painted on the window. Two men in business suits stepped out the front door of the title company, carrying briefcases, and got into the back of the limo.

Twenty minutes later the limo stopped outside the press entrance to a giant sports stadium, but only Blanco and Jeffries got out.

"West Ham versus Chelsea, eh?" the driver asked Joe.

"What?" Joe asked.

"You're going to the football match, West Ham versus Chelsea," the driver clarified.

Joe looked to Frank. "I guess we are."

"Not through that gate," Frank said, pointing to a sign over the entrance through which Jeffries and Blanco were passing. "It says Press and Authorized Personnel Only."

"I guess we'll have to buy tickets and try to find them inside," Frank said, paying the driver and getting out.

"Looks like we'll be lucky if there are any left for sale," Joe said, walking quickly toward the long line at the ticket window.

The boys were lucky enough to get two of the last tickets.

"We might as well be in Scotland, these spaces are so

far away," Frank said, taking back his ticket stub from the turnstile attendant.

"We're sure not going to find Blanco and Jeffries if we go to our assigned spaces," Joe agreed.

"We'd better not split up," Frank recommended. "We'll never find each other again."

Joe nodded and they headed toward the sections closest to the field.

Frank looked up at the sea of humanity, standing and cheering. "This will be like trying to find a needle in a haystack," he remarked, then turned his gaze toward the field.

The game was in full swing, and a West Ham player had just placed the ball in the corner of the field closest to the Chelsea goal.

"That's John Moeller taking the corner kick," Joe said.

Moeller kicked the ball toward the players massed in front of the Chelsea net. One of his teammates headed the ball, which deflected off the goalie's fingertips and into the Chelsea goal.

The crowd erupted. Someone grabbed Joe and swung him around in celebration while Frank got bumped against the man walking behind him by some other rowdy fans.

"They take this seriously," Joe said after he had been put down. "Too seriously."

"Man, that was a perfect kick, though," Frank commented.

"Not perfect," a white-haired man in a cap said.

131

"Moeller's perfect kick came in a World Cup match he played for England three and a half years ago. The corner kick hooked perfectly over the goalkeeper and into the far side of the net."

Frank looked back at the game as Chelsea started their attack. A sign at the far end of the field caught Frank's eye. It appeared to be an advertisement for a restaurant called the Corner Kick.

"Looks like they even named a restaurant after Moeller's play," Frank said, nodding toward the sign.

"That's because John Moeller owns it," the man in the cap told him. "It's huge, one of the most popular restaurants in London. Packed all the time, it is."

Pieces of the puzzle began falling into place in Frank's head.

"If I'm caught, you can forget about the Corner Kick," Frank said aloud.

"What?" Joe said, still scanning the crowd.

"What Shah said on the phone," Frank explained. "I have a hunch he was talking to Jeffries. Blanco wasn't there to talk about renting the theater for a show. I think he was there to talk about buying the theater and turning it into another Corner Kick restaurant!"

"Wow, Frank, that really seems to fit," Joe agreed. "Jeffries was talking about room for dancing in the restaurant, not on the stage!"

"No wonder Moeller has been in that neighborhood," Frank added.

"But why would Jeffries take such drastic measures to stop our show? Why wouldn't he just let *Innocent*

Victim have its run and then sell the theater to Moeller and Blanco?" Joe wondered.

"Good question, Joe," Frank said. "I don't have an answer."

The Hardys spent the next ninety minutes scouring the stadium for Jeffries. Only a minute remained in a tied game.

"Wait, there they are!" Joe shouted, pointing to Blanco and Jeffries, ten rows up near midfield. Jeffries saw Joe and jumped to his feet, exchanging a few quick words with Blanco before heading down the steps toward the field.

The Hardys headed down after him just as a Chelsea player kicked the winning goal as time expired. The rowdy crowd leaped up in an angry eruption, then many began rushing toward the exits.

The boys got stuck between two gangs of rival fans shouting and threatening one another.

"Forget Jeffries for now!" Joe yelled. "We'd better get out of here!"

A young woman fell to the ground in front of Frank as they tried to escape the mayhem. Frank helped her to her feet, but then got pushed from behind and hit the pavement as a throng of fans began to trample him beneath their feet.

15 Stampede!

Frank covered his head with his arms and tried to get up, but the force of the solid mass of people pushing from behind knocked him down again.

Someone grabbed Frank by the back of his jacket and started dragging him along the ground. It was Joe, who pulled Frank to his feet.

"Over here!" he shouted as he and Frank jumped onto the railing of a concrete wall over a tunnel leading from the field. Frank and Joe breathed sighs of relief as they were now out of the way of the throngs stampeding from the stadium.

Below in the tunnel, the losing West Ham United team was headed for the locker room. "It's John Moeller!" Joe yelled, spotting the winger trotting past reporters and photographers toward the tunnel.

"We've lost Jeffries. Maybe we should drop in on Moeller," Frank suggested.

"You mean literally?" Joe asked.

"Literally," Frank replied. "Drop!"

Frank hung off the railing and dropped onto the pavement of the tunnel eight feet below. Joe followed a second behind him.

"Mr. Moeller!" Frank shouted to the soccer star as he approached.

In a flash, the Hardys were set upon by security guards, who roughly escorted them away from the West Ham team and down a hallway.

"Timothy Jeffries is a criminal. You're being deceived!" Joe shouted.

Joe's accusation got Moeller's attention momentarily, but then he moved on with his team.

Frank swallowed hard as he looked into the holding cells filled with roughneck fans who had been brought here for fighting and other bad behavior. Some had dried blood on their faces, and none of them looked too friendly.

"Hold on!" a voice called from down the hall. John Moeller had returned. "I want to talk to these boys."

The security guards released the Hardys, who then followed Moeller into a locker room filled with reporters and a lot of tired, disappointed players headed for the showers.

Frank quickly explained the sabotage that had been

occurring at the Quill Garden Theatre and how they believed Timothy Jeffries might be involved.

"How did you know I was planning to open the Corner Kick II?" Moeller wondered. "Mr. Blanco and I have been keeping it a secret."

"Then Mr. Blanco is your business partner?" Joe asked.

"Yes," Moeller replied. "But we were led to believe the Quill Garden Theatre would be vacant by next week so that we could close the sale and begin renovations."

"Well, let's say someone's been trying to *make it* vacant for you," Joe remarked.

"Why the rush to buy it and build?" Frank asked.

"The World Cup!" Joe blurted out, remembering his conversation with Dennis Paul at the pub two days earlier.

"Yes, that's right," Moeller said. "We want to have the grand opening during World Cup competition when England will be teeming with football fans."

"Did you give Jeffries a deadline?" Frank asked.

"We had two other sites we were considering if the Quill Garden deal didn't go through by next weekend," Moeller told them.

"So Jeffries had a window of opportunity to turn a huge profit on a rundown theater for which he had paid next to nothing," Frank deduced.

"If he could get *Innocent Victim* out of it pronto," Joe added.

"Interesting theory, boys," Moeller said. "If it's true, I'll not be buying the Quill Garden Theatre, I promise you."

At that moment Blanco walked into the locker room with a big smile on his face. "Good news, John," he told his partner. "Jeffries dropped his price, and we closed today!"

"Closed!" Moeller exclaimed.

"Yes, it was all signed, sealed, and delivered in the limousine on the ride to the stadium," Blanco said. "I thought Jeffries would enjoy coming down here to meet the team, but he said he had pressing business."

"Yeah, getting away," Joe commented.

"You didn't give him any money, did you?" Moeller asked.

"Yes, the down payment was in cash, as he requested," Blanco replied. "One hundred and fifty thousand pounds."

"Jeffries knows we're onto him, he might take that money and run," Frank guessed.

"Where was Jeffries headed?" Joe asked Blanco.

"I don't know, but there would be no getting a taxi with this crowd," Blanco said, perplexed. "Chances are he headed for the tube."

Racing out of the stadium, the Hardys followed the crowd to the nearest tube stop. The platform was jammed with fans who began filing onto a train that had just pulled into the station.

Frank knew Jeffries could easily have boarded the train without being spotted. "Make the call, Joe. Do we get on this train or wait?"

The train doors began to close.

"Get on!" Joe yelled, and he and Frank squeezed

through the door and stood, smashed against the glass in the packed train car.

At each stop Joe slipped out to see if he could spot Jeffries getting off the train, then hopped back on when the doors began to close.

"No luck," he told Frank.

After several stops the train reached the stop for the theater. Joe asked, "What do we do?"

"I guess we get off and call Detective Inspector Ryan," Frank replied.

The boys stepped off the train and were headed for the way out when Joe suddenly grabbed Frank and pushed him behind a trash bin.

"Jeffries!" Joe whispered. "I just saw him."

"Is he headed up the escalator to the exit?" Frank asked.

Joe peeked around the edge of the bin. "No, he's switching to the Hammersmith line."

"Let's go," Frank instructed, moving from behind the trash bin.

"I'll grab him," Joe said as they hurried down the tunnel to the Hammersmith line, "and you—"

"We're not ready to grab him yet," Frank said. "There's a lot of evidence to be sorted out and a lot of accusations that need to be proven. Besides, I want to know where he's headed with that money."

The boys waited, out of sight, until Jeffries boarded a Hammersmith-bound train, then rushed into the car next to it.

Jeffries got off at Baker Street, and the boys followed

him to Madame Tussaud's Wax Museum. Jeffries purchased a ticket and went inside.

"Joe, call Chris on his dad's cell phone," Frank instructed. "Tell him to contact Detective Inspector Ryan and meet us down here. Meanwhile, I'll buy two tickets."

Joe nodded and then hurried to a nearby pay phone.

"The museum closes in thirty minutes," the woman in the ticket booth warned Frank.

"Thank you, thirty minutes will be plenty of time," Frank said, purchasing the tickets anyway.

Joe met Frank and they entered the museum together. Even though he was pursuing a criminal, Joe couldn't help but check out the incredible, lifelike exhibits as he passed by them.

One room had wax figures of movie stars such as James Dean, Humphrey Bogart, and Marilyn Monroe, while the next contained likenesses of the British royal family.

Frank kept a sharp eye on Jeffries, who moved through the crowded museum as if he were rushing to catch a flight at a busy airport. He finally stopped and sat on a bench next to a woman who had dozed off.

For a moment Frank wondered if the woman was faking it, and might be Jeffries's contact. Then he realized that she was made of wax!

Frank and Joe moved behind a talking figure of Elvis Presley, as Jeffries's eyes darted around the room looking for someone. Suddenly he rose to his feet and walked down a ramp leading to the Chamber of Horrors.

The Hardys followed at a safe distance. The dimly lit

Chamber of Horrors pulsated with eerie sounds and music, punctuated by occasional screams that echoed through the dark corridors.

Wax figures of victims were arranged in tortured poses behind bars on each side of the corridor.

"Pretty gruesome, huh?" Frank whispered to Joe.

"It sure is," Joe replied quietly. "We need to come back when we have more time."

Jeffries stood in a small, dark alcove beside the likenesses of Marie Antoinette and King Louis XVI, their bloody wax heads stuck on spikes on each side of a guillotine. A museum guard with short black hair walked over to Jeffries.

"Neville Shah!" Joe said under his breath.

Opening his briefcase, Jeffries discreetly removed a stack of British currency and handed it to Shah.

"Go back to the entrance and find Chris and Detective Inspector Ryan," Frank told his younger brother. "I'll keep an eye on these two."

Joe headed back up the winding ramp. Shah and Jeffries began walking Frank's way, so he ducked down a side corridor.

As Frank reached a service door, he turned back to see if Jeffries was following. Someone suddenly stepped through the service door and grabbed him, slapping a powerful hand over his mouth and yanking him into the darkness.

16 Chamber of Horrors

"You should have stayed in America," Frank's attacker snarled, putting Frank in a choke hold and dragging him down a narrow hallway into a cold storage area.

Out of the corner of his eye Frank could see that it was Corey Lista and elbowed him in the ribs. Lista released the choke hold, but then drove Frank against the wall. Frank fell, stunned, toppling over someone standing beside him.

In the red glow from an emergency light, Frank saw a face, half eaten away on one side. The overhead lights suddenly came on, and Frank realized that he was looking at wax.

"This is where we bring the rejects," Shah said to Frank with a smile. "The waxworks that are obsolete."

"So this is your part-time job, eh, Neville?" Frank asked, playing it cool.

Shah just smiled. Jeffries stood by the light switch, glaring at Frank.

"How did he get here?" Jeffries demanded of Lista.

"I wager that he followed you," Lista replied, pulling Frank to his feet.

"Where's your brother?" Jeffries asked.

"I lost him at the soccer game," Frank lied.

"How often does anyone come in this room?" Jeffries asked Shah.

"They won't be altering any exhibits for at least three days," Shah replied.

"Plenty of time for us to be off and away," Jeffries said, then turned back to Frank. "So many sights in dear old London you'll miss. If only you could have behaved as a normal tourist, I should say we would all be a great deal happier right now."

"Instead, we will become outlaws on the lam," Lista said, "and you will become the only *Innocent Victim* they write about in the newspaper."

"This has gotten so out of hand," Jeffries sighed. "I was just trying to sell a white elephant of a theater for a little profit."

"A giant profit, you mean," Frank said, checking out of the corner of his eye for some means of escape.

"Whatever the amount, you must admit it wasn't worth what you've put us through," Jeffries said. "Or what we are about to put *you* through."

Frank saw an arm, lying on the ground to his left. In

one swift movement, he snatched it up and swung, catching Lista under the chin.

The wax limb snapped in half, but it had done the trick. Lista backpedaled and slammed into the opposite wall.

"Frank?" came a muffled call.

"In here!" Frank shouted at the top of his lungs,

Shah and Jeffries took off down the corridor and into the Chamber of Horrors. Dazed, Lista tried to follow, but Frank tackled him to the ground.

A moment later Joe rushed in with Detective Inspector Ryan and another officer. Ryan immediately cuffed Lista's hands.

"Corey Lista?" Joe said surprised. "Where are Jeffries and Shah?"

"I thought you would have passed them," Frank said, jumping to his feet.

"They must have gone on through the Chamber of Horrors," Detective Inspector Ryan said, putting Lista into the other officer's custody.

"What's beyond the Chamber of Horrors?" Frank asked Chris.

"The gift shop and the exit," Chris replied.

The Hardys, Chris, and Detective Inspector Ryan raced after their quarry, passing through the gift shop and out to the street in time to see Neville Shah pulling away from the curb with Jeffries in his passenger seat.

Detective Inspector Ryan ran to his own car, and Chris and the Hardys got in. "Here now, you can't come with me."

"Hurry or you might lose them!" Frank exclaimed.

"I'm dropping you off the first chance I get!" the detective protested, then floored it.

They chased Shah's car across London, around Big Ben, along the Thames, and past the Tower of London. Near St. Katharine's Dock, Detective Ryan cut in front of Shah's car and drove him into the curb.

Shah and Jeffries fled the vehicle, with the theater owner still holding his briefcase of money.

"The two suspects are on foot, headed toward St. Katharine's Dock," Detective Inspector Ryan radioed in.

The passenger side of the detective's car was jammed against Shah's, so the boys scrambled out the back door.

Jeffries and Shah split up. Jeffries continued toward the marina, while Shah headed for the Tower Bridge.

"I'll go after Shah!" Joe shouted. "You guys stay with Jeffries."

Jeffries was by far the slower runner, and Frank and Chris were within fifty yards of him when he reached the dock.

As a river tour boat shoved off, Jeffries jumped, barely making it onboard. By the time Frank reached the edge of the dock, the boat had moved too far away.

"Stop!" Frank yelled. But between the loud engine and the guide talking over the public address system, no one heeded his shouts. For the moment Jeffries had gotten away.

Neville Shah pushed aside the attendant at the entrance to the first tower. Joe Hardy's eyes widened in disbelief as Shah jumped a rail and began climbing the steep, sloping spans leading to the top of the first tower of the Tower Bridge.

Joe knew he couldn't follow "Anacro, the Human Spider" that way, so he took the stairs inside the tower and raced up until he reached the glass enclosed walkway one hundred and forty-five feet above the Thames River.

Joe spotted Shah scuttling along the top of the enclosed walkway looking much like a spider. Joe ran across, passing beneath Shah and reaching the second tower before he did.

Joe unhooked a boundary rope and ran up some steps to an off-limits area at the very top of the tower. He unhooked and opened some shutters, giving Shah a way into the tower from the outside.

Having set his trap, Joe waited, catching his breath and hoping he would be the spider and not the fly.

Shah's feet swung through the open window and he dropped to the floor. When Shah sprang to his feet, he was greeted by one of Joe Hardy's powerful punches.

The Human Spider's head rocked back, his knees buckled, and he dropped to the ground, unconscious.

"Guess the Human Spider had a glass jaw," Joe said to himself.

By the time Frank, Chris, and Detective Inspector Ryan reached Joe, the younger Hardy had bound Neville Shah with a rope used to keep tourists out of restricted areas of the tower.

"This was not my idea," Shah pleaded, having re-gained consciousness. "Mr. Jeffries hired me," he confessed to Detective Inspector Ryan.

"Well, if you're willing to tell me all about Mr. Jeffries and the Ghost of Quill Garden," Detective Inspector Ryan said, "I'm certain we can offer you a lighter sentence."

"Where is Jeffries?" Joe wondered.

"He escaped," Frank said, frowning.

"Hardly," Detective Inspector Ryan said, stepping on to the scenic walkway and pointing down. "There's his boat docking. And there's half a dozen of my mates from Scotland Yard waiting to greet him."

The men looked like ants from the top of the Tower Bridge. But Joe smiled as he saw six ants converge on one ant as it tried to run from the crowd of ants getting off the tour boat.

"It's over, lads," Chris said, patting his American friends on the shoulders. "Let's get back to the theater."

Mr. Paul sank into his third-row seat, stunned by the story the Hardys and his son had told him. "Incredible," Dennis Paul remarked. "However, I'm afraid there's one part of this mystery you haven't solved. Where is Jennifer Mulhall and our light board?"

Joe shook his head and frowned, concerned. He heard the faint tapping of the pipes from the heating system. Then it struck him what the tapping sounded like. "Shave and a haircut."

"What?" Frank asked.

"The heating pipes are tapping out the cadence of 'Shave and a haircut, two bits,' " Joe explained.

Frank listened. "You're right!"

The Hardys followed the tapping until it got incrementally louder.

"I got it!" Frank exclaimed, getting a hunch where it was coming from. "Mr. Paul, can I borrow your keys?"

Frank took the keys and ran up to the light booth with Joe and Chris behind him. Taking the back stairs, he stopped at the first door the Hardys had come to when they explored the theater the night the lights had exploded.

"Remember, Joe, Jennifer's chain didn't have a key that fit this lock," Frank said. "I'm certain Mr. Paul won't have this key either."

"Let's try the old-fashioned way," Joe said.

Frank and his brother backed up and charged the door, slamming their bodies into it. On the third try, the lock broke and the door gave way.

The Hardys found themselves in the old furnace room. Sitting on her knees, with her mouth and hands bound with electrical tape, was Jennifer.

Joe pulled the tape away from her mouth. "Jennifer!" he said, giving her a hug.

"It took 'Shave and a haircut,' did it?" Jennifer asked. "I've been tapping on that pipe all day!"

"Here's your light board," Frank said to Chris, then he pulled a white satin sheet and something akin to a wedding veil from beneath it. "And here's Lady Quill's ghost, as played by Timothy Jeffries."

"Right. It was Jeffries you saw in the light booth that night," Jennifer said. "That other door over there leads right into his office."

Electricity was in the air five nights later as opening night of *Innocent Victim* drew to a close. Chris Paul uttered his last line, Jennifer faded the lights down, and the audience erupted in applause.

The Hardys stood, giving Emily Anderson and Chris a standing ovation.

Frank turned to Schulander, seated next to him. "Didn't you like it?"

"I loved it," Schulander said, "but I only stand for my own shows. On the other hand, it might be one of my shows someday. I'd like to talk to Dennis Paul about moving it to a bigger theater."

With that, Schulander rose to his feet to join in the standing ovation.

"One thing still doesn't make sense," Joe spoke to Frank over the applause. "Jeffries owned Quill Garden for only five years, but people have been claiming to see the ghost of Lady Quill for more than a century."

Frank shrugged, continuing to clap. "That's one of those mysteries of the theater."

Frank smiled, and Joe smiled back. The younger Hardy looked up at the private box where Dennis Paul sat beaming as he listened to the audience applaud his work. Through the red curtain at the rear of the box, Joe saw a figure in white watching the stage.

"Frank," he said, tapping his brother on the arm. "Look!"

But when Joe turned back, the figure was gone.

"What?" Frank asked.

"Nothing," Joe said. "Just another mystery of the theater."

NANCY DREW® MYSTERY STORIES By Carolyn Keene

A MINSTREL® BOOK
Published by Pocket Books

THE HARDY BOYS® SERIES By Franklin W. Dixon

It's TV—in a book!
Don't miss a single hilarious episode of—

Don't Touch that Remote!

Episode 1: Sitcom School
Spencer's got his own TV show!
Watch him try to keep his wacky co-stars out of trouble!

Episode 2: The Fake Teacher (November 1999)
Is that new teacher all he seems?
And is Jay hiding something really, really big?

Episode 3: Stinky Business (January 2000)
Danny's got a brand-new career, and something smells!
Here's a clue: It ain't fish!

Episode 4: Freak Week (March 2000)
It's the spookiest show ever as the gang spends overnight in their school.
Will Pam's next laugh be her last?

Tune in as Spencer, Pam, Danny, and Jay negotiate the riotous world of school TV. Laugh out loud at their screwball plots and rapid-fire TV-style joking. Join in the one-liners as this over-the-top, off-the-wall, hilarious romp leaves you screaming—
Don't Touch That Remote!

A MINSTREL BOOK

Published by Pocket Books

2302